DAKOTA
KNOX
& THE
ARCHAEOLOGY
THIEF

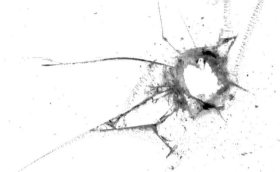

Dakota Knox & the Archaeology Thief
is a work of fiction. The characters, heist, and details
regarding the museum's security procedures, alarm
systems, vault, and data center are fictional. Any
resemblance to actual events or persons, living or
dead, is entirely coincidental.

DAKOTA KNOX & THE ARCHAEOLOGY THIEF

DAKOTA KNOX & THE ARCHAEOLOGY THIEF

CHARLIE H. CAMPBELL

FACTS:
- All descriptions of archaeological artifacts
- References to events in the Bible, the writings of Flavius Josephus, and other historians

CHAPTER 1
Wednesday, June 8, Jerusalem.

It was a quiet night for the police department in Jerusalem, but peaceful nights don't always end that way. Wednesday morning, at 3:05 a.m., a police dispatcher's voice broke the radio silence. "We need all available officers in Jerusalem to make their way to the Israel Museum. Security reported a power outage at the museum and the theft of one of its most valuable archaeological artifacts."

In response to the urgent call, several police officers raced through the empty streets to the museum.

Back at police headquarters, the sergeant sounded off. "Wake the detectives! Set up checkpoints on every road out of the city! Alert airport and marina officials and tell them to be on the lookout. And call Chief Weisner."

"What did they steal, sergeant?" an officer inquired.

"An ancient stone slab, about 3,000 years old. I just did a quick search about it on the Internet. It's called the Tel Dan Stele, more popularly known as **the David Inscription**. There's an inscription in the stone that mentions King David in the Bible. It's been on display at the museum for years. And now it's gone!"

• • •

As the sun warmed the city a few hours later, reporters and camera crews set up outside **the museum** for a 9:00 a.m. televised press conference.

At 9:05, the police chief walked out the museum's front doors to speak to the reporters. Mordecai Weisner was 58 years old. He wore a dark navy-blue suit over a light blue police uniform shirt with two colorful ribbon bars across the top of his left pocket. He stood at a wood podium, flanked by Daniel Denenberg, the museum director, and several police officers.

"Thank you, ladies and gentlemen, for your patience and for being here this morning. I am Mordecai Weisner, Chief of Police. At approximately 2:15 this morning, the Israel Museum lost power. Normally, the museum's backup system takes over. Unfortunately, it failed to activate."

Some reporters groaned.

Weisner cleared his throat and resumed. "Police detectives

continue their investigation, but there *is* evidence that the power failures were the result of foul play. We'll have more on that soon. But according to our initial interviews with museum security, the security guards continued to patrol the museum property after the power went out."

"How could they see?" one of the reporters asked.

Seriously? Weisner wondered. He locked gazes with the reporter. "Flashlights, sir. Maybe you have one at home."

Some in the crowd laughed.

"As I was saying, according to the museum's chief of security, his team continued their rounds through the museum, keeping an eye out for any signs of criminal activity. At 2:55 a.m., they noticed that the stone slab that mentions King David was missing. They immediately called police headquarters and alerted us of the apparent theft."

"Chief Weisner," a female reporter interrupted. "I'm with i24 News. I'm familiar with that artifact; it's behind thick glass or maybe Plexiglas. Was there broken glass in front of the display case?"

"No."

"Chief Weisner, thank you for briefing us on this," a male reporter said. "I'm with TV7 Israel News. Were alarms triggered anywhere on museum property?"

"Not that we know of. The power failure and what may have been a sophisticated computer hacking appears to have disrupted the security systems."

A woman reporter from Israel News Network said, "Chief Weisner, are you looking into the possibility that the museum's security guards were involved in the robbery?"

Daniel Denenberg, who ran the museum and knew the

security guards personally, immediately shook his head no.

"No one is outside the bounds of our investigation," Weisner answered. "Unfortunately, the security cameras throughout the museum stopped functioning when the power went out. So, we may not have video of the theft. But our detectives are in the museum's data center seeing if there is video from earlier in the day."

"It seems preposterous that someone could take all the cameras offline," a reporter from the *Jerusalem Post* said. "Will the security cameras on the buildings near the museum be examined?"

That question is preposterous, Mordecai thought. He sighed and said, "Yes, of course."

"I hope so," the reporter mumbled.

Weisner rolled his eyes and continued. "We know this is a big story, folks. We appreciate your patience as the investigation continues. You can rest assured that we will do all we can to apprehend the culprit and recover the missing artifact. Thank you."

He started to back away from the podium, hoping to cut the press conference short and rejoin the investigation, but a dozen hands flew up.

"Police Chief!"

"Chief Weisner!"

"When can we expect . . ."

He reluctantly stepped back to the podium and pointed to someone from *The Times of Israel*. As the reporter asked his question, a man walked out of the museum through its glass doors. He made a beeline to Weisner, whispered something in his ear, and handed him a piece of paper. Weisner silently read it.

The reporters' eyes were glued to his facial expressions for clues. He didn't disappoint. His eyes widened as he read. Then he shook his head. He set the paper down on the podium, looked up, and said, "Ladies and gentlemen, I've just been informed that power has been restored to the museum, and sadly four other artifacts are missing. Museum curators, working alongside our detectives, have determined that the following artifacts are gone: the Pontius Pilate inscription; **a stone box that mentions Caiaphas**, the high priest; the first-century heel of a Jewish crucifixion victim, and perhaps the most troubling . . ." He paused. His heart ached to complete the sentence.

Mordecai grew up going to synagogue every Saturday. Although his heart had grown cold toward his parents' religion, he knew the significance of the artifact he was about to mention. He slowly let out a long breath as if blowing out a candle.

"The 2,100-year-old **scroll of Isaiah**. The museum's most treasured Dead Sea Scroll is gone."

Several reporters gasped.

"This is heartbreaking news," the chief said. "The Isaiah Scroll is Israel's Mona Lisa, perhaps the most important cultural treasure of the Jewish nation. But I assure you, and those of you watching at home, that we . . ." A loud **helicopter** approached overhead. So he yelled out the remainder of his sentence, "We *will* get to the bottom of this!"

All questions were on hold—the helicopter was deafening. Weisner squinted to get a better look. The chopper belonged to the police department. It landed on a spacious flat area around the backside of the building. When the rotor noise subsided, reporters bombarded Weisner with more questions.

"What might the motive have been?"

"We don't know this early on."

"How might the thief or thieves have broken into the museum?"

"We don't know yet."

"Are there any suspects?"

"We can't comment on that at this time."

After a couple of minutes of this back-and-forth, they were interrupted again by a noise above them. It wasn't the chest-rattling noise of an incoming helicopter but more of a high-pitched buzzing sound. Weisner and the others looked up as it approached. It was a drone coming in from the west about 200-feet high. Weisner was able to make out some details as it slowed down near the museum. Unusually large, its black octagon-shaped body looked about 5-feet-wide with several angled edges. Above the drone's body were six propellers, one at each end of six arms that extended a couple of feet from the drone. The arms each had small blinking red lights on their tips.

The reporters resumed questioning the police chief. Mordecai was deaf to their questions. All he could think about was the drone. *That's not a police drone, and it's not an Israel Defense Force drone!*

It passed over their heads, stopped, and hovered about 150 feet above the museum's new state-of-the-art data center. It was a two-story stone and glass building about 100 yards away from the press conference. Weisner and several reporters walked closer to get a better view.

"I don't like that thing," Weisner muttered to himself. Fearing the worst, he turned to a couple of officers next to him and said, "Men, have your guns ready." As he spoke, a panel on the bottom of the drone slid open. Four gray cylinders rolled out and fell toward the roof of the data center.

"Oh God!" Weisner shouted, "Get down!" Reporters and camera crew scrambled for cover. Weisner turned and ducked behind a concrete trash receptacle. Seconds later, the building exploded. Chunks of stone and shards of glass whizzed past the trash can. The noise was deafening.

Weisner poked his head around the side of the trash can to assess the situation. Peering through the smoke and dust, he saw that the structure was a smoldering pile of jumbled stones and burning office equipment. The air reeked of burning plastic and pulverized electronics. A few people nearby were crying and asking for help.

Daniel Denenberg, the museum director, was lying on his side about 20 yards away from the police chief. His nose was bleeding, and he was covered in dust.

"Daniel! Are you okay?" Weisner yelled.

"I'm alive. I'm okay."

"I'm going to see who I can help."

As the drone continued hovering over the ruins of the data center, a few officers ran toward it, firing at it with their 9mm handguns. Their flurry of bullets did nothing. The drone was too high. The few bullets that reached it ricocheted off, hardly leaving a mark.

As Weisner tended to an injured cameraman, he radioed one of his commanders. "Doesn't anyone have a rifle?"

"We're looking for one, Chief."

"Tell the helicopter pilot to return to the chopper with a couple of guys. And if the drone sticks around, maybe they can get up there and have a better shot . . . or at least track where it goes."

It was too late. Whoever was flying the drone turned it toward the helicopter and unloaded about fifty bullets through its windshield, engine, and rotor blades.

The commander came back on the radio. "Uh, Chief, did you see that?"

No answer.

"Chief? Are you there? The chopper is toast, Chief."

Weisner didn't respond. He *did* see it and could hardly believe his eyes.

As smoke billowed out of the helicopter, the drone soared straight up about a thousand feet and flew off to the west.

Weisner was relieved that it was gone but astonished at what he just witnessed. He reached for his phone and called police headquarters. "Johanna, connect me to General Ackerman with IDF. Quickly, please."

"Yes, Chief, I'm on it. How are things going at the museum? Is the David Inscription really missing?"

"A whole building is missing, Johanna!"

"Oh dear."

"The general, Johanna, get me the general."

"I'm working on it. Just waiting for a response and a secure connection."

Weisner brushed off the dust and bits of glass on his jacket as he waited. Behind him, police officers and others tended to the injured. He held his hand over his phone and yelled, "Stay away from the helicopter—that thing could blow!"

"Mr. Weisner," Johanna said, "you're connected with General Ackerman."

"Good morning, General Ackerman. This is Mordecai Weisner, Israel Police Chief. Have you seen the news?"

"About the museum theft?"

"Yes."

"I'm just getting word of it. Tell me more."

"Several valuable artifacts were stolen from the **Israel Museum** early this morning. And a couple of minutes ago, an unmanned drone dropped a cluster of bombs on the museum's data center and lit up our chopper with a hail of gunfire. Pardon my frustration, General, but what on God's green earth is going on? How did a large armed drone move so freely through Israeli air space?"

"I'm turning the TV on."

"Please do. Every news channel is down here covering the story."

"You're there now, Mordecai?"

"Picking chunks of glass out of my hair as I speak, sir."

"Listen carefully," the general said, "I want you to make sure . . ."

Weisner couldn't hear a word the general said. Ambulances and fire engines started streaming into the museum's parking lot, sirens blaring, making it impossible to hear.

"I can't hear you, General. It's too loud! Let me walk inside."

When Weisner entered the museum, the general was no longer on the line.

"Of course! . . . Johanna, get the general back on the line."

While he was waiting, Daniel Denenberg walked by.

"You look like a train wreck, Dan. Glad you're okay."

"Thanks. I think I'm going to retire earlier than I planned."

"Hold off for a couple of weeks. We'll need your help to track down these losers."

SEVEN WEEKS EARLIER
ENCINITAS, CALIFORNIA

Chapter 2
Friday, April 22, Encinitas, California.

Seventeen-year-old Dakota Knox was perfectly positioned for one of the largest waves of the day at **Swami's**, a popular surf spot in Encinitas, California. His friends shouted, "Yeah! Go, Dakota!"

He spun his surfboard around. "All right, boys, I'm taking this wave in." It was a solid 8-foot wave that peeled south. With every carving turn, Dakota sent gallons of water flying over the back of the wave. His friends hooted and hollered for him when the wave finally died out.

"Stoked!" Dakota yelled into the air. "That wave was insane!"

He waded through the whitewash and made his way up the long flight of wooden stairs that led to the parking lot. He was content to call it a day. Three hours of surfing had left his lips parched and stomach growling.

When he reached the top of the bluff, Dakota bumped into a classmate in the parking lot. "Hey, Josh! You heading out?"

"Yeah, just got off work. The waves are firing, huh?"

"Yeah, it's super fun out there."

"How'd your new board work?" Josh asked.

"Awesome! I like it."

Dakota worked at a surf shop close by Swami's and had been given a new experimental surfboard to test out. The manufacturer said the board was constructed with materials that made it fifty times less susceptible to dents and breaking than an average board.

"The board looks amazing!" Josh said. "What's it made of?"

"I don't know. It's sort of top-secret for now. But the company said the material is stronger than Kevlar."

"Isn't that what they put in bulletproof vests?"

"Yeah," Dakota said.

"Maybe it will help you survive a shark attack or something."

"Maybe! Well, it was great to bump into you, Josh! I'll see you at school on Monday. Have fun out there!"

Dakota placed the surfboard in a rack on the side of his beach cruiser. As he pedaled across Pacific Coast Highway, he thought about how blessed he was to live a few minutes from the ocean. *Thank You, God, for spring break, the beach, and the fun waves today. And thank You that summer is almost here. I'll have three months to surf and relax before I head off to Liberty University in the fall.*

He parked his bike on the side of his family's house and rinsed off his light brown hair in their outdoor shower.

"Is that you, Dakota?" his mom Abigail asked.

"Hey, Mom!"

"How were the waves?"

"So fun. What's for dinner?"

Abigail laughed. "I'm doing good, too."

"Sorry, Mom. How are *you*?"

"Great, thanks for asking. We're having **carne asada tacos**, rice, and beans. Should be ready in about ten minutes."

"You're the best. Thanks, Mom."

Dakota dried off, went inside, and walked upstairs to his bedroom. He paused as he walked past a mirror in the hallway. *Whoa! I forgot to put on sunscreen. My nose and cheeks are sunburned.* He looked closer at his blue eyes. *It feels like I have a grain of sand in my eye. . . . There it is! Got it.*

He walked into his room and picked up his acoustic guitar. He sat on the edge of his bed and played chords to some of his favorite songs by Switchfoot and Jack Johnson.

A few minutes later, Dakota's dad William called to him. "Hey, Dak! Dinner's ready."

"Coming!"

He walked downstairs and joined his parents, brother, and sister around the granite island in the kitchen.

As they prepared their plates, Dakota said, "Hey, Dad, how was work today?"

"Good! But I'm ready for the weekend. How was your day?"

"Amazing! The waves at Swami's were pumping."

"Nice. Did you catch some good ones?"

"Tons."

Abigail brushed aside a strand of her wavy brown hair and asked, "Are you guys going to youth group tonight?"

"For sure. Hank, you coming?"

Hank gave a thumbs up. He was Dakota's fourteen-year-old adopted brother. His real name was Hwan, but he preferred to be called "Hank."

As they enjoyed their meal together at the dinner table, William said, "I have something I want to run by you guys."

Dakota had heard that line several times over the years. And he knew it meant something significant was about to drop.

"An Israeli defense firm offered me a temporary job in Israel. They're developing a new laser-based interception system, and they asked if I could help them over the summer."

"You lost me, Dad," Jalynn said. She was Dakota's ten-year-old adopted sister. "They're developing a what?"

"It's a military defense system that shoots down incoming missiles with lasers."

"Ah, like Star Wars!" Hank said.

"Sort of. Do you guys remember a few months ago when the news showed Hamas and Hezbollah attacking Israel with hundreds of missiles?"

"Yeah, that was so lame!" Dakota said as he took a bite of his taco.

His dad nodded. "For sure. Well, Israelis defend themselves by shooting down those missiles. But they shoot them down with their missiles that cost about $50,000 each. That's a huge expense. Well, a defense firm called Light Shield is developing a system that uses high-powered lasers to shoot down the mis-

23

siles instead."

"Wow, that's awesome!" Hank said.

"It would save Israel billions of dollars. And because lasers travel at the speed of light, Israel could take out a larger number of incoming missiles much faster. Anyhow, they're looking for a couple of scientists with expertise in the field of high-powered lasers. So, they reached out and asked if I could come and help them."

Dakota said, "That sounds cool, Dad. You should go."

Abigail smiled at William a bit nervously, knowing what he was about to propose.

"I want to, Dak, but I think we should *all* go. Another scientist who already committed to going is bringing his whole family. I thought that sounded like a great idea."

Jalynn clinched both fists, raised them, and pulled them down as though a significant victory had just occurred. "Going!" she said. Jalynn hadn't done much traveling in her brief ten years, but if the trip included a flight, she was up for it.

"Does Israel have beaches with waves?" Dakota asked.

"Yes," his dad replied, "and the water is 84 degrees during the summer!"

"That's cool."

"You mean *warm*," Hank said.

"Clever, Hank. What else is there to do?" Dakota inquired.

"Well, we could explore sites mentioned in the Bible, visit museums, go to the Sea of Galilee, rent ATVs. There are a plethora of fun things to do."

"And I heard the food is duhlishush, too!" Hank tried to say with a full mouth.

"Yes! They have wonderful food there, Hank."

Dakota smiled. He loved his Korean brother, Hank. The Knox family adopted him twelve years earlier after a drunk driver killed his parents. The Knoxes had been good friends with them. When William and Abigail learned that Hank would be put into foster care, they decided to adopt him. Dakota was five at the time and was thrilled to have a little brother join the family.

Dakota asked his dad, "Would we stay in a hotel for three months?"

"No. Light Shield, the company that offered me a job, said they'd put our family up in a beautiful house that's close to the beach. It's amazing! Check this out." He showed the family some photos on his phone. "That's the front of the house. The inside is fully furnished with nice furniture and beds. The backyard has a beautiful pool with a waterfall and slide. There's a mini-movie theater, a game room with a pool table. Here's the trail that leads down to the beach."

"Going!" Jalynn exclaimed again. She turned and gave Hank a high five. "Hold on, Dad. Do they have a Disneyland there?"

"No, no Disneyland," he said, chuckling.

"Still going!"

Dakota loved his black sister as much as Hank. His parents adopted her when she was three. They had been caring for her as foster parents for what was originally a three-month commitment. When it became clear that her birth mother could no longer raise her, they happily adopted her.

Dakota leaned back in his chair. "Dad, a couple of minutes ago, you said hundreds of missiles are being fired at Israel. That sounds sort of sketchy—all of us living there for three months."

Hank shook his head and rolled his eyes. "Don't be a chicken."

"I'm not afraid," Dakota replied. "I'm more concerned about Jalynn and Mom."

"I'm sure we'll be safe," his dad said. "Most of the missiles that Hamas and Hezbollah fire aren't even capable of reaching the area where we'd be living. And Israel can shoot down most of them. Also, the missile attacks only seem to happen every few years, and there's nothing serious happening at this time."

Abigail asked William, "Isn't there an underground bunker in the house, too?"

"Yes! There is."

"Will you quit your current job at ALS, Dad?" Hank asked.

William Knox was a highly regarded scientist and engineer at Advanced Laser Systems in San Diego and had worked there since 2010.

"No. My boss gave me permission to take three months off. He loves the Jews and knows I can help them. So, I'll still have my current job when we return."

"All right, Dad. You make the call," Dakota said. "I'll be okay with whatever you and Mom decide. I was planning to surf this summer and relax before I start at Liberty, but if Israel has waves and some fun things to do, I'm up for it."

Hank and Jalynn nodded enthusiastically.

Abigail said, "I love you three! Thanks for being open to this. It's a wonderful opportunity for Dad to be a help to the Jewish people. And we've talked about going to Israel for years. I think it will be fun. Life-changing."

Dakota stood and headed toward the sink to clean his plate.

"We need to get going. Youth group starts in 20 minutes."

Dakota and Hank hopped in their parents' white Chevrolet Tahoe and headed off to church. They loved Friday nights with their church friends, skate ramps, volleyball games, outdoor firepits, s'mores, times of worship, and encouraging teachings from the Bible.

Abigail looked at William with a huge smile on her face. "I guess we're going to Israel! The kids are more open to it than I expected."

"Yeah, they are. I'm amazed! Let's go for it. I'll email Light Shield tonight and let them know."

"Honey," Abigail said, "this is going to be an unforgettable summer."

"It sure is."

Chapter 3
Thursday, May 12, Israel.

Radomir Lucic looked out the window of his twin-engine jet.

The pilot's voice came in over the speakers. "Mr. Lucic, we're beginning our descent into Ben Gurion Airport in Israel. We'll have you on the ground in approximately 15 minutes.

Local time is currently 11:35 a.m."

Radomir Lucic was a 67-year-old billionaire. His father was Serbian. His mother was British. They were killed in a plane crash when Radomir was 23. Being their only child, he inherited all their homes, stocks, and businesses. Not having the skills or desire to manage any of it, he sold everything and walked away with a massive fortune.

Radomir slid his plate and utensils aside. He turned toward the back of the jet. "Dario, the omelet could use more cheese next time."

Dario was Radomir's full-time chef. He apologized and tried to explain that the jet's refrigerator was low on cheese.

"Manage the supplies better then," Radomir said. He reclined his white leather seat and wrapped his thick fingers around the back of his shaved head. He looked at his iPhone sitting on the table in front of him and said, "Hey Siri, call Ahmed." Ahmed was Radomir's righthand assistant.

Siri didn't respond.

Radomir raised his voice a bit. "Hey Siri, call Ahmed!"

No response.

Radomir leaned forward, grabbed his phone, and screamed, "Siri, I hate you! Call Ahmed this stinking second, or I'm going to destroy you!"

"I'm sorry, I don't under . . ."

Radomir hurled the phone against the wall near the front of the cabin. Dario watched from the kitchen at the back of the jet.

"Dario!" Radomir yelled, "Call Ahmed for me . . . now!"

The short Italian quickly dialed Ahmed's number and handed his phone to Radomir.

Ahmed answered. "Hey, Dario, what's up? Is big guy treating you okay?"

"Big guy?"

"Is that you, Dario?"

"No. This is your boss, Radomir, using Dario's phone."

"Oh, Mr. Lucic. I'm so sorry. I meant 'big' as in head honcho or boss, not—"

"Stop. Dario and I will be touching down in about ten minutes. I'm sure you'll be waiting for us at Arrivals. Yes?"

"I'm here waiting for you. We'll be . . ."

Radomir ended the call and reached for his hat. It was a **gray Homburg**, a felt hat with a narrow-curled brim.

After they landed, Radomir and Dario walked to the airport's Passport Control. An Israeli agent asked to see Radomir's passport.

"Country of origin?" the agent inquired.

"England."

The man slowly thumbed through Radomir's passport. "Where'd did you fly out of?"

"London Farnborough Airport."

"Why are you here?"

"I'm a philanthropist. I'm meeting—"

"A what?"

"A philanthropist. Someone who donates money to good causes. That's why I'm here. I'm meeting with the heads of non-profits that I'm considering partnering with."

"Interesting. Where will you be staying?"

"Ritz Carlton. Tel Aviv."

The agent stared at Radomir. "There is no Ritz Carlton in Tel Aviv."

Radomir's heart rate spiked. His assistant Ahmed had told him to say the Ritz in Tel Aviv. He fumbled for words. "Um . . . uh . . . I was told that's where the Ritz is."

"It's actually in Herzliya, immediately north of Tel Aviv. Close enough. How long will you be staying?"

"Planning to leave next Thursday."

"Very well. Go your way. Enjoy Israel."

He tipped his hat to the agent and, with his British accent, said, "I will. Good day!" Radomir walked off, breathed a sigh of relief, and thought, *that philanthropist line works every time.*

Radomir was not a philanthropist. He was a liar, and he had come to Israel for one reason: his insatiable obsession with acquiring archaeological artifacts for his private collection.

Radomir's love of history and archaeology began in his fifth-grade classroom. In his twenties, that love grew into an unquenchable desire to own books on ancient history. In his thirties, it led him to crisscross the globe visiting museums. In his forties, it morphed into a passion for acquiring his own artifacts. But in his fifties, after he bought a sprawling 18-room mansion in England, his lust to acquire artifacts mutated into an unsatisfiable obsession. He convinced himself that every wall, shelf, and fireplace mantel needed an ancient artifact.

Radomir's collection of artifacts wasn't to impress people who came to his estate. He never invited anyone inside his house except those who worked for him. The artifacts were for him. He loved to look at them and touch them. In the evenings, he'd light candles, turn off the lights, and sit in his **leather recliner**. He'd close his eyes and hold an artifact close to his face, slowly breathe in through his nose and savor the artifact's scent. For a few minutes, he'd sit there in silence, visualizing himself as a hero in a historical scene related to the artifact. Then he'd have imaginary hours-long conversations with Alexander the Great, Nebuchadnezzar, Cleopatra, and other well-known persons from history.

Radomir was an unusual man, but he was shrewd enough to know that purchasing artifacts lawfully was the wisest way to avoid trouble and enlarge his collection. "But that's where the problem lies," he often said to himself. "The museums that hold the artifacts I want are never going to sell them." So, with the hired help of museum insiders, he stole them.

His conscience troubled him after the first couple of heists. But he snuffed out the condemning thoughts by convincing himself that the museums' employees didn't care for the artifacts like he would. He would cherish them. He would love them and give them a wonderful home. And that is why he came to Israel. It was time for another heist.

• • •

Radomir and Dario walked into the Arrivals Hall at the airport. Ahmed and Eeman, Radomir's bodyguard, greeted them. They had arrived in Israel on Radomir's yacht two days earlier.

Ahmed had been an administrator at the Egyptian Museum in Cairo, and Eeman had worked as a security guard at the Iraq Museum in Baghdad. After they helped Radomir "relocate" artifacts from the museums, he persuaded them to move to England and work for him by offering them pay raises, new identities, and a taste of his billionaire's lifestyle: nice clothes, private jets, expensive cars, yachts, and excellent meals.

The four men exited the airport and walked toward a black **Range Rover** in the parking lot. Dario looked up at Eeman. "Sheesh, I forgot how tall you are, Eeman—you're like a giant!"

Eeman smiled. He was six-foot-five-inches tall, with broad, muscular shoulders and black curly hair.

The men settled into the SUV and drove off.

"Ahmed, were you able to secure a house?" Radomir asked.

"Yes, I think you're—"

"What city is the house in?"

Ahmed could sense by Radomir's tone that there was a problem. He said, "It's in Herzliya, right near the beach. It's a beautiful house, Boss."

Radomir's tone got tenser. "Why then would you tell me

that we were staying in Tel Aviv?"

"Oh, yeah, that was a tiny mistake, it's actually—"

"You fool!" Radomir yelled.

Ahmed cringed in the front seat. Even though he was 32 and stronger than his boss, Radomir was seated directly behind him. Ahmed envisioned Radomir reaching his pudgy hands around the headrest and strangling him. He had choked him in the past, and Ahmed thought it was only a matter of time before he'd do it again.

"I might have been detained or refused entry," Radomir said.

"I'm sorry, Boss."

"If you ever do that again, I'll have your house torn down, and you can walk back to Egypt."

"It won't happen again."

Ahmed dreaded losing his job and having to move back to Egypt. He enjoyed the lifestyle that working for Radomir had given him, even though he thought Radomir was a royal pain.

After twenty minutes of silence, Radomir said, "I like these new Range Rovers. Do I own this?"

"We rented it," Ahmed said. "Well, *I* didn't rent it. Some guy named Hamadi did."

Ahmed had more than a dozen fake identities with matching passports, credit cards, and driver's licenses. Everything he purchased or rented during an "artifact relocation project" was with a different identity. This made it difficult for authorities to track their movements.

When they pulled up to the **ocean-front house** in Herzliya, Radomir said, "Show me to my room. I'm going to take a nap. And Dario, I'd like dinner at 8:00 p.m. That's my normal

6:00 p.m. dinner time in England."

"What can I bring you?" Dario asked.

"Grilled fish, garlic mashed potatoes, and asparagus sound good."

"Dessert?"

Radomir tilted his head and stared at Dario. He thought back to the time when he met Dario in Naples, Italy. Radomir had visited the National Archaeological Museum there and then dined at a 5-star restaurant. The food was delicious, and Dario was the executive chef. Radomir talked him into working for him in England for substantially more pay.

Still looking at Dario, he asked him, "How long have you worked for me?"

"Almost a year, Boss."

"What have you learned in that year, Dario?"

"You *always* want dessert."

"I always want dessert."

"What shall I prepare for you?"

"Surprise me with something."

"But—"

Ahmed quickly interjected. "Dario will be happy to surprise you, Boss. Enjoy your nap."

Dario hated when Radomir said, "Surprise me." Once, he brought him a large slice of Key lime pie, and Radomir threw it against the wall and said he hated limes. On another occasion, he brought him a bowl of chocolate and peanut butter ice cream, and Radomir went on a rampage accusing Dario of trying to kill him with an allergic reaction to peanuts.

After Radomir shut his bedroom door, Eeman said, "Just make him that sticky toffee pudding. He never complains about that. Just don't leave out that teaspoon of vanilla extract. We know what happened the last time you did that."

• • •

That evening, after Radomir finished his toffee pudding, he got up from the table and walked outside to the white stone patio. He watched the sun go down over the Mediterranean Sea and walked back inside. Looking at Ahmed and Eeman, he said, "We'll scout out the museum in Jerusalem tomorrow morning. Plan to leave here at 9:30 a.m."

"Sounds good, Boss," Ahmed said.

Radomir loosened his belt to make room for the food he'd eaten. "Ahmed, why are we staying so far from the museum? It's nearly an hour's drive away."

"It is, Boss, but we need to be close to the yacht. That **marina** to the south of us is where your boat is docked. You can probably see it. This house works perfectly."

"Ah, yes, I do see it. I love that boat."

Ahmed and Eeman had sailed *Poseidon's Dream* from Italy, where it had been moored, a couple of days earlier.

"Is the drone still on the boat?" Radomir asked.

"No. It's in the garage."

"How'd you get it to the house?"

"Eeman and I disassembled it in Italy, packed the parts in duffel bags, and carried them to the Range Rover after we docked."

"Very good. I'm headed to my bedroom for the night. Goodnight, men."

Chapter 4
Friday Morning, May 13, Herzliya, Israel.

After breakfast, Radomir, Ahmed, and Eeman drove to the Israel Museum in Jerusalem. Dario stayed behind to tend to the yacht and prepare dinner. Radomir's goal in going to the museum was twofold: scout out the museum for new artifacts and look for a man he could pay to help him steal them.

Radomir had the recruitment process down to an art and could usually find a person within a day or two.

When they arrived at the museum, Eeman parked the SUV and looked at Radomir. "You want me to come in with you unarmed or stay out here and keep watch?"

"Come in. I'll be fine."

Eeman placed his Smith & Wesson .45 caliber handgun in the SUV's console. He hated to leave it behind, but the museum had metal detectors.

After purchasing their tickets, the men headed through the doors to the museum's outside garden and walkway.

"All right, men, you know the routine," Radomir said.

Ahmed stopped and pulled out his phone. "Hello. Ah, yes, how are you? I was expecting your call . . ."

As they continued walking, Eeman whispered to Radomir, "He could win a Grammy for his acting, couldn't he?"

Radomir looked at Eeman. "No. Grammys are for *music*. You meant an Oscar."

"Who's Oscar?"

"Never mind. Follow me."

Radomir and Eeman walked into the massive archaeological wing of the museum.

Ahmed stayed outside, still pretending to be on a phone call. As he meandered around the property, he discreetly videoed details about **the museum**.

Inside the museum, Radomir breathed in deeply and exhaled. "Museums have a certain quality about their air. I love this place already!"

Near the entrance was a display of seven standing clay coffins unearthed south of Gaza in 1972. They dated back to around the 14th century BC and were about six feet tall. As Radomir and Eeman walked around opposite sides of the coffins, Eeman heard Radomir whisper to himself, "One of these would look fantastic next to the fireplace in the northwest guest room on the second floor."

Eeman thought, *No one ever goes in there. You haven't had a guest spend the night since you bought the place ten years ago!*

When they met on the other side of the coffin, Eeman whispered, "Hey Boss, remember that whatever artifacts you pick out have to fit in our crate."

"Remind me what size it is."

"It's only 1.2 meters. These coffin things are too big."

"Yeah, you're right. Maybe we'll get one some other time. I really like these."

Every ten or fifteen feet, Eeman heard Radomir say, "Oh, I like this one" or "I wish it wasn't behind glass. I'd love to touch

it . . . or smell it."

Eeman thought Radomir's obsession with artifacts was very strange.

As planned, they slowly drifted apart. Radomir had more success recruiting museum insiders when he approached them alone.

• • •

A few minutes later, Radomir spotted a bored-looking museum employee. He buttoned up his navy-blue suit jacket, adjusted his gray hat, and walked over to the man. "Excuse me, sir, what a terrific museum! I just love it. You must enjoy working here."

The man, in his sixties, shrugged. "Yeah, it's okay. It doesn't pay the bills, but—"

"The pay isn't very good?"

"I'm a volunteer. I don't get paid anything. But I love my country. I'm retired. I want to help people understand our—"

"You're a wonderful human being," Radomir told him. He shook his hand and continued walking. *He's not the guy.*

A couple of minutes later, Radomir approached another employee, a man in his forties. "Excuse me, sir, what a lovely museum. I'm just amazed by these exhibits. You must love working here."

"I *do* love working here," the man said.

"All right," Radomir said, "well, you keep up the great work."

Around the corner, Radomir bumped into another employee. "Excuse me, sir, what an amazing museum! It's just incredible. You must enjoy working here."

"Not really," he said. "To be honest, it's exhausting being on my feet all day."

"Oh yeah, I can imagine. That would be awful. But you're paid well?"

"No, they hardly pay me anything."

"Let me ask you, do these archaeological discoveries strengthen your faith in God or the Bible?"

"Absolutely! There are a lot of discoveries here that—"

"Excuse me. I'm so sorry. My phone just vibrated, and I was expecting a call. It was a pleasure to chat with you." He pretended to talk to someone until he was out of the man's view.

After an hour of strikeouts, Radomir saw an employee leaning against a wall, looking at his phone. He was about twenty-five years old, with black hair pulled back in a ponytail. Radomir walked up to him. "Excuse me, young man, what a cool museum. I just love it. You must enjoy working here."

"No. I don't, actually."

"The pay's not very good?"

"The pay's okay."

"Why don't you like working here?"

"I work here because my dad said he was going to kick me out of the house if I didn't get a job and cut back on video games. But I couldn't find a job."

"But you got a job here!"

"Well, because my dad's the director of the museum."

"Oh, I see. So, you're working here just to have a bedroom at your parent's house. There's no fun in that. You deserve better pay so you can buy your own place—a nice house!—and a fast car."

"For sure! This job sucks."

"Do any of these archaeological discoveries strengthen

40

your faith in God or the Bible?"

"Are you kidding me? The Bible's a collection of legends and myths. I'm an atheist. I trust in science."

"I agree with you, young man. You're very wise. What's your name?"

"Avner."

"I'm Robert." Radomir never used his real name with people until he trusted them.

"Nice to meet you, Robert."

"I'm sorry, Avner, but I didn't catch your last name."

"Denenberg. Avner Denenberg."

"It was a delight to chat with you, Avner. I wish you all the best." Radomir adjusted his hat, walked away, and said to himself, "Bingo!"

A couple of minutes later, he reconnected with Eeman and Ahmed. "We can go. I found our man."

"I'm still filming," Ahmed whispered. "I'm getting the inside now."

"All right, you keep doing that. Eeman and I will be at the café. I don't need to talk to anyone else."

Chapter 5
Friday Afternoon, May 13, Israel.

When Radomir, Ahmed, and Eeman left the museum, Ahmed asked his boss, "What's the guy's name?"

"Avner Denenberg. He's discontent and angry about his current circumstances. Feels he's underpaid. He's also an atheist, and his dad is the director of the museum. Perfection!"

Ahmed pulled out his phone, opened Instagram, and did a search for an Avner Denenberg. After a bit of scrolling, Ahmed showed his phone to Radomir and said, "Is this him? He lives in Jerusalem."

"That's him."

"His account is private," Ahmed said, "but that's not a problem."

Eeman laughed. "Time for Geneviève to come out and play."

"Exactly," Ahmed said.

Geneviève wasn't a real person, but no one would know by looking at her Instagram account. Ahmed had created it a couple of years earlier to contact male museum employees, flirt with them, and inquire about getting their help. The account had a profile picture of an attractive woman. And Ahmed had populated her feed with several stolen photos of lattes, smoothies, inspirational quotes, a golden retriever, and thoughtful captions. And it had proven to be an effective bait. Men often responded in the affirmative.

Ahmed switched over to Geneviève's account, found Avner, and pressed "Follow."

Twenty minutes later, as they were still driving, Ahmed said, "There it is! Avner approved Geneviève's request and followed her back. He's on the hook."

Eeman was giddy. "It works every stinkin' time. These idiots are so gullible!"

Radomir shook his head and rolled his eyes. "If I recall correctly, Eeman, this is the same way Ahmed hooked you."

"Oh yeah. That's right," Eeman acknowledged, looking a little embarrassed.

After dinner, Ahmed sat on the **white couch** in the living room. He looked out toward the sea and typed his first message to Avner:

> Hi Avner! My name is Geneviève. You don't know me personally, but you helped me find an artifact at the Israel Museum a few weeks back. I remembered your name from your name badge and thought I'd reach out to you and see if you'd be interested in getting coffee sometime.

Ahmed put his feet up and said, "Geneviève has reached out to Avner."

Ten minutes later, Ahmed sat up. "Avner responded."

"That was fast!" Eeman said.

Ahmed read it.

> **Avner:** Hi Geneviève. I'd love to get coffee. Where would you like to meet?

Ahmed looked at Radomir. "We've got a live one!" He typed a response from Geneviève:

> How about Café Bezalel in Jerusalem?

> **Avner:** Sure. I love that place.

Geneviève: So do I. Hey, would you mind if we switched over to the Signal app to finish making plans? I don't like messaging on Instagram.

Avner: I like Signal, too. Elon Musk recommended it.

Geneviève: Great! Here's my account name . . .

A couple of minutes later, they resumed their conversation on Signal:

Geneviève: Hey Avner!

Avner: Hey!

Geneviève: Why don't we meet on Monday at 8 a.m.

Avner: That works for me.

Geneviève: Wonderful. Hey, I'd like to ask you about something else.

Avner: Sure.

Geneviève: I'd like to know if you'd be interested in helping me relocate a few archaeological artifacts from the Israel Museum to another site.

Avner: Relocate?

Geneviève: Yes, I'd like to move a few artifacts from the Israel museum to another location.

Avner: Umm . . . that sounds like stealing. So, no. Are you an undercover cop? What is this, a setup?

Geneviève: It's not a setup, Avner, and I'm not a cop. And you wouldn't be stealing anything. Your role would only involve placing a few artifacts inside a wood crate, after hours, during a power outage that my team would set in motion, and then wheeling the crate outside. So the artifacts would still be on museum property. After that, you could head home a rich man. My team would take the artifacts from there.

Avner: There are cameras everywhere. It's impossible.

Geneviève: It's not impossible. We've done this before. My team will take out the power to the entire museum. That will take the cameras offline. We're also going to destroy the data center's hard drives, so there won't be any video footage of your involvement. We'd be willing to pay you very well for your help.

Avner: How much?

Geneviève: $500,000 USD in bitcoin per artifact with a budget of two-to-three million dollars.

Avner: Seriously? I could do a lot with that.

Geneviève: I'm serious. I can send you $25,000 USD in bitcoin right now to show you how serious I am.

Avner: Okay. My wallet address is below. If the money lands in my wallet in the next hour, maybe I'll trust you, and we can continue the conversation.

Geneviève: If you decide not to help, I'll expect you to return the money.

Avner: I can do that.

Geneviève: Great. I'll send it in a couple of minutes.

Ahmed looked at Radomir, who was falling asleep on the couch. "Hey Boss, I need your approval for Geneviève to send $25,000 to Avner as a gesture of good faith."

"Send it," Radomir said. "And surprise him—add an extra $10,000."

"Will do."

With a few taps on his phone, Ahmed transferred the money to Avner. Twenty minutes later, Avner messaged back:

Wow! You weren't messing around. The money came through. But you transferred $35K. Was that a mistake? I can return the extra 10K. Let me know.

Geneviève: Not a mistake. My boss said to throw in an extra $10K. You can keep the $35K as a down payment if you'd be willing to help us.

Avner: Well, I was suspicious about this being a sting operation, but the more I think about it, the more I'm convinced that law enforcement would never try to pull off a sting that involved moving priceless artifacts.

Geneviève: Right!

Avner: The chance that they could be damaged would make them off-limits. So I believe your offer is legitimate. I'm willing to help. Where do we go from here?

Geneviève: Well, I'm so happy to have your help, Avner :). What's your phone number? My boss will reach out to you soon to discuss which artifacts he'd like and more details.

Avner: Here's my number . . .

Geneviève: I'm looking forward to meeting you for coffee.

Avner: So am I, Geneviève!

Ahmed set his phone down and said, "Avner's in!"

"Woo! The heist is on!" Eeman yelled. "I love me a good heist. Ahmed, do you remember that one in Turkey? The car chase? So fun!"

"Of course."

Radomir stood. "I'm off to bed. Fine work, Ahmed."

Chapter 6
Saturday, May 14, Herzliya, Israel.

The following day after breakfast, Radomir walked over to a leather chaise lounge in the living room, laid down, and dialed Avner's number.

"Hello."

"Avner, this is Geneviève's boss, Robert."

"Oh, hi!"

"I talked to you yesterday at the museum. I was wearing a navy suit with a gray hat. Do you remember me?"

"I do."

"I couldn't discuss these matters with you at the museum for obvious reasons. But I'm happy to hear you received the money last night and that you're willing to help us."

"I did receive the money. Thank you."

"Of course. And there could be a lot more coming your way soon. Geneviève explained that we'd like your help putting some artifacts in a crate for us."

"Yes. Which ones are you interested in?" Avner asked.

"The best ones. The David Inscription. That's a must."

"That's a good one. What else?"

"The Isaiah Scroll."

"Ooh, that one will be tough—it's locked up in a vault. The one on display in the museum is a replica."

"I trust that you can get your hands on the combination for the vault. Your dad is the director of the museum. I'm sure he has the codes."

"I'm sure he does," Avner said. "Where there's $500,000,

there's a way."

"Yes! That's the attitude I like."

"What else?" Avner asked. "I'm writing these down."

"Well, let me ask you this, Avner. You work at the museum. What artifacts are most popular?"

"Hmm. . . . There are three artifacts that are a big draw for Christians. The Pontius Pilate inscription, Caiaphas's ossuary, and the heel bone of a first-century crucifixion victim. Tour guides stop their groups and discuss those three every day."

"Yes! I saw those when I was there. Those are the ones I want."

"Are you a Christian?" Avner asked.

Radomir laughed. "Oh God, no. But those are well-loved artifacts, and that makes them more attractive to me. Those five should fill up our crate."

Avner said, "That's five artifacts at—"

Radomir finished his sentence. "$500,000 each."

"That's 2.5 million dollars," Avner said.

"You're good at math Avner."

"Why, thank—"

"When you come through for us, I'm going to pay you with bitcoin. It makes it harder for investigators to trace the money. Are you fine with that?"

"Sure."

"Good! Well, Avner, it's a pleasure to have you on the team. If you can document for us that you're making progress on things, we can send you an advance payment."

"Progress?"

"For example, if you can show me that you've got the code for the vault and that it works, we'll advance you $100,000. We want you to know we're serious and that the money is there to pull this off. Once the heist is complete, and we have all the artifacts in our possession, I'll pay you the remaining balance."

"Perfect. I'm wondering about a couple of things, though, Robert."

"Like?"

"Geneviève mentioned a power outage. That will be crucial. But the museum has a backup power supply to keep the cameras and alarms working."

"It won't on the night of the heist," Radomir said. "My assistant is going to take down both systems. He's a whiz. We're also going to blow up the data center. And that will destroy the museum's hard drives and any archived video footage."

"All right. But I'd prefer no one is hurt."

"Yes, of course. There shouldn't be anyone in the data center in the middle of the night."

"How are you going to get the artifacts off museum property?"

"We're going to use a drone. My assistant will discuss the specific details with you as we get closer, but we're going to fly the crate out with a drone."

"Uh, that's not going to work. You guys must not live here. Israel has an amazing weapons system that detects and shoots down unauthorized unmanned aircraft. Your drone will be blown out of the sky."

Radomir laughed. "You haven't seen our drone. Our drone is made from a new material that makes it nearly undetectable to current systems. And it also has jamming capabilities to confuse any system that tries to interact with it. Its body is heat-resistant to lasers and practically bulletproof. So we're not concerned about Israel's defenses."

"Wow. Okay. What about the weight of the artifacts and the crate? That's a lot of weight. What kind of drone can—"

"Avner!" Radomir yelled. He was losing his patience. "If you'll wheel the crate outside, we will not have a problem picking it up. We have already thought all this through."

"Okay."

"My assistant Ahmed will coordinate more details with you soon. He'll also help you get a plan in place to distract the nighttime security guards. Everything will come together very nicely."

"Where are you going to take the artifacts?"

"I like you, Avner, but I can't tell you that."

"I understand. When do you want to pull this off?"

"We're planning for the first week of June. Will that be enough time for you?"

"For sure."

"Avner, you're going to be part of one of the biggest heists in Israel's history! And afterward, you're going to be able to buy a nice house and car, and really begin to live! And Geneviève is excited that you're able to help us."

"Oh yeah?"

"Oh yeah!"

"We're getting coffee Monday morning!"

"Yes, she told me. I think she likes you."

"Oh wow. That's exciting."

"Well, it's nice to talk to you, Avner. My assistant Ahmed or Geneviève will be in touch soon."

Radomir set his phone down and looked at Ahmed. "Nice guy. Make sure Geneviève postpones her coffee date with him."

Chapter 7
Sunday, May 29, Encinitas, California.

The month of May flew by for the Knox family. Dakota graduated from high school. Hank finished ninth grade, and Jalynn, fifth. They packed their suitcases, said goodbye to friends and family, and headed off to the San Diego Airport. After an 18-hour flight that included a two-hour stop at JFK airport in New York, they landed at Ben Gurion International Airport about 28 miles northwest of Jerusalem.

Monday, May 30, Israel.

As the Knox family walked through the terminal, Dakota said, "Wow. This isn't what I was expecting. I thought the airport would be sort of old and outdated."

His mom Abigail said, "I love it! It's so modern and welcoming. There are lots of restaurants, coffee shops, and art exhibitions. And check out that waterfall coming down from the ceiling."

Dakota's dad William discreetly pointed at three armed soldiers in the terminal and said, "This airport is considered one of the safest airports anywhere in the world."

As they waited for their suitcases, Dakota noticed a middle eastern man in his forties standing on the other side of the baggage carousel. He was staring at the Knox family. Dakota wondered why. *Does he know who my dad is? Is it because my parents are white, and Jalynn is black? Or Hank is Korean? Get over it, man.*

Dakota didn't want to think the worst, but he was in a foreign country and thought, *I need to be alert*. He had already thought about the possibility of someone wanting to hurt his dad because of his work with Light Shield. *So,* he thought, *if that guy tries anything, I'm going ballistic*. Dakota was a strong six-foot-two-inch-tall teenager with two years of Krav Maga training, a self-defense and fighting system that includes a combination of techniques found in boxing, wrestling, judo, aikido, and karate. He didn't want trouble, but he wasn't going to let anyone lay a finger on someone in his family without a fight.

Dakota couldn't take the staring any longer. He looked straight at the man and quickly tilted his head back a little as if to say, "What? You have a problem?" As he did that, someone behind him tapped his back and said, "Hey!"

Dakota spun around, ready to confront whoever it was.

"Whoa!" his dad said.

"Oops. Sorry, Dad!"

"That's okay. Keep an eye out for our bags. I need to find our driver. I thought he was going to meet us at baggage claim with a sign that says, "Welcome, Clark Family.""

"Who are the Clarks?" Hank inquired.

"Shh," William whispered. "That's us. For our safety, Light Shield didn't want to put our last name on the sign. So *Clark* boys, grab our suitcases when they come out."

Their dad walked away to search for the driver. Dakota spun back around to see if the man was still there. He wasn't. *Where'd he go? Did he follow my dad?* Dakota walked around a bit and scanned the crowd of travelers, but the man was gone.

Dakota and Hank began removing their suitcases as they

arrived at the carousel.

Their dad returned a couple of minutes later, talking on his phone. "Okay, we'll see you in there after we clear Customs. Thanks." Rejoining the family, William said, "I had it wrong. Our contact is meeting us in the Arrivals Hall."

When the Knoxes walked into the hall, a man in his thirties wearing a gray suit approached them with a sign: "WELCOME CLARK FAMILY!"

"That's our guy!" William said.

The man recognized them. "Greetings! Welcome to Israel. My name is Uri Berenson." He lowered his voice and looked around. "I'm with Light Shield." Uri shook their hands and said, "I hope you had a good flight. We have two vans outside, one for you with some water and snacks inside, and another for your luggage." He looked at the long black bag hanging off Dakota's shoulder. "What do you have in there?"

"This is my guitar."

"I'm sorry. The other bag."

"Oh, this is my surfboard."

"Ah, yes. I heard there was a surfer in the family. Wonderful. Maybe you can give me a lesson sometime."

"Sure."

"The beach where you'll be staying is nice. You'll be glad you brought your board." He asked if he could help with some of the luggage and said, "All right, everybody, follow me—my new friends, all the way from California! We are truly honored to have you work with us, William. Our team is thrilled to have your help."

Uri led them outside to two silver vans. After the suitcases were loaded, they made their way to Herzliya, an affluent city on the coast of the Mediterranean Sea about 20 miles north-west of the airport.

When they arrived at the house, a tall wooden gate rolled open, and the Knoxes got their first glimpse of the front of the house.

"Sweet!" Jalynn said. "This place is amazing!"

The modern-looking home was two stories tall with white and gray walls and a smattering of natural wood features. The lush foliage all around the property was lit up beautifully.

As they got out of the vans, Dakota wondered why two brand-new **Ford Broncos** were in the driveway. One was dark red, and the other was dark gray.

"Is there another family staying here?" Dakota asked Uri.

"No."

"Whose cars are these?"

"These are for you guys to use, compliments of Light Shield."

"Whaaat?" Dakota turned to his dad and said, "Look at these new Ford Broncos! These things are sick."

"Very nice," His dad agreed. William looked at Uri. "That's too kind of them. Thank you!" Turning back to Dakota, he

whispered, "One for me and one for Mom."

"I can drive one occasionally."

"We'll see."

The Light Shield drivers unloaded their suitcases and wheeled them to the porch. Uri unlocked the front door and handed the keys to William. "Welcome to your new home away from home, Knoxes. It's fully furnished and all yours for the summer."

Uri gave them a short tour of the house and showed them how to work the alarm, climate controls, spa, and so on. The Knoxes were blown away. The house was better than they had imagined. It was a six-bedroom, 5,000 square-foot home about 100 yards from the ocean in a quiet neighborhood.

An eight-foot-tall white wall surrounded the property except on the side facing the ocean. On that side, there were a variety of palm trees and tropical plants. In between the plants were a couple of paths that led out to a bluff and down to the beach. The backyard looked like an island paradise. It had a **lagoon-style pool** with a large waterfall that flowed off a rock ledge. Built into the rocks surrounding the pool were three fire features whose flames lit up the backyard and added to the tropical ambiance. In the pool, behind the waterfall, was a cave. And built into the boulders making up the waterfall structure was a slide with water running down it.

"Pinch me, Mom! Is this a dream?" Jalynn asked.

Abigail smiled. "It's not a dream, Jay. God has blessed us beyond measure."

"Dad! Look at all this stuff," Dakota said. "Bodyboards, stand-up paddleboards, beach cruisers, chairs, umbrellas, towels . . ."

"Feel free to use it all," Uri said. "The CEO of Light Shield, who owns the house, told us to stock the house with anything we thought you'd enjoy. Come. I'll show you the game room next."

As they walked by the spacious kitchen with its marble countertops, Uri said, "You shouldn't have to go grocery shopping for a few days. We stocked the refrigerator and the pantry with fruit, vegetables, meats, cheese, bread, eggs . . ."

Dakota turned to his mom, who did the bulk of the grocery shopping, and gave her a fist bump. "You love that, Mom."

"Best news I've heard all week!"

The game room on the second floor had a pool table, foosball table, ping pong table, air hockey table, dartboard, an Apple HomePod to stream music, and a refrigerator stocked with several kinds of sodas and juices.

"I know where I'll be hanging out," Hank said.

"I'll leave the bedrooms for you guys to check out," Uri said. "But there's one more place I need to point out—the bomb shelter. You probably won't need it—this part of Israel is very safe—but you should at least know where it is."

Uri led them down a hallway on the house's first floor. He bent down to a barely noticeable latch in the wood flooring and pulled up a door. Beneath it was a black spiral staircase that led down to a room.

As the Knoxes went down the stairs, Abigail whispered, "I hope we never need this room."

The windowless white walls were decorated with framed photographs of Israeli beaches. The room had two gray couches, a coffee table, two wood end tables with lamps, three bean bags, a widescreen TV on the wall, a bathroom with a shower, and a light blue retro-looking refrigerator stocked with a variety of drinks and non-perishable snacks.

When they were done looking at the room, Uri said, "Well, you guys must be exhausted after that long flight. You can explore the rest of the house on your own. If you enjoy working out, there's a gym on the second floor at the end of the hall. And you have my cell number."

As they walked out the front door, Uri said, "Call me anytime if you have any questions or need anything. I live about two minutes away, and I'm at your service." As he drove off, he hollered out the window, "Enjoy those Broncos!"

"I will!" Dakota yelled back. His dad looked at him. "I'm kidding, Dad!"

"All right, everyone, let's head in," Abigail said. "We need to get unpacked, teeth brushed, and get to sleep."

When they walked inside, William said, "I'm not sure how to shut the gate at the bottom of the driveway. Did Uri show anyone a button or clicker?"

"No," Abigail said. "You'll figure it out, honey."

"This neighborhood looks safe," Hank said. "It's not like anyone's going to attack us the first night we're here, Dad!"

Chapter 8
Tuesday, May 31, Herzliya, Israel.

Dakota rolled out of bed the following day and pulled open the thick white curtains covering his second-floor bedroom window. He slid the window open and felt the warm Mediterranean air drift into his room. *It feels like a dream to wake up on the other side of the planet.*

He walked down the hallway to see if Hank and Jalynn were awake. They were.

"Hey guys, I'm going to explore the beach. Want to come?"

"Let's go!" Jalynn said.

Hank wasn't quite as eager but agreed to tag along.

They walked down the trail on the bluff that led to the beach. At the bottom, Jalynn said, "I'll race you guys to the water!" and took off.

The boys followed, but Jalynn was too fast.

When they reached the water, Dakota said, "Wow! It feels like a bath."

"And look at these cool shells!" Jalynn said.

The three of them walked south along the water's edge for about a mile. They admired the beachfront homes and a pod of dolphins swimming close to the shore.

Dakota felt his phone vibrate. He reached for it in the front pocket of his shorts and read a text message from his mom:

> I'm making pancakes, and Dad cut up fruit. You guys hungry?

Dakota: We're on our way!

"Let's head back, guys," Dakota said. "Mom made pancakes!"

• • •

When they were back at the house enjoying breakfast, William said, "So, what do you guys think? Pretty cool property, huh? Did you explore the beach?"

"Yeah, Dad, this place is awesome!" Dakota said. Hank and Jalynn nodded in agreement. "White sand. Warm water. There's a path from the backyard to the beach. About a mile south of here is a marina with a bunch of docked boats."

"I'm glad you guys like it!" their dad said.

As they were finishing their pancakes, there was a knock on the front door. William, Abigail, and Dakota looked at each other.

"Uh, Dad, I thought you were going to shut the gate last night," Dakota said.

"I wasn't able to."

Dakota wondered, *Could it be the man I saw at the airport? Did he track us here?* He slid his chair back and said, "I'll get it."

"Look out the peephole, please," Abigail said.

Dakota peered through the hole in the door. "It looks like a friendly family on the porch."

Hank rolled his eyes. "Probably Jehovah's Witnesses."

Dakota opened the door.

A man wearing shorts and a t-shirt, who looked to be in his late forties, said, "Hello there!" He reached out his hand to shake Dakota's. "My name's Steven Hansley. This is my family.

We're your next-door neighbors."

"Oh! Hello. It's nice to meet you. My name's Dakota."

The man's wife asked, "Are your parents home?"

"They are." Dakota turned and loudly said, "Hey Mom and . . . Oh, they're right here." The whole family had come up behind him. "This is my mom, Abigail; and dad, William; my brother, Hank; and sister, Jalynn."

They exchanged smiles and handshakes.

Steven Hansley said, "This is my wife, Nicola. And these are our three kids: our daughter Afton, son Ethan, and daughter Evelyn." He explained that they had arrived in Israel two days earlier and that he was the other scientist that Light Shield had hired for the summer.

"Oh, wow!" William said. "This is wonderful."

"We were looking forward to meeting you all," Abigail said. "But we didn't know you'd be living next door. That's terrific! Please, won't you come in and sit down?"

As they walked in, Nicola Hansley said, "Light Shield offered to put us in the house next door. It's beautiful, like this one. The CEO owns both homes. We live in London, pretty far from the beach. Steven and I thought this would be a great way to spend the summer. Our daughter Afton wasn't excited about leaving her friends right after graduating from high school, but we assured her that it was going to be a wonderful time."

As the adults continued discussing Light Shield and the helpful contributions Steven and William were hoping to make, Dakota said, "Hey guys, why don't we give our parents some time to get to know each other. And, if it's okay with you, Dad, we'll go play pool or something."

William smiled and nodded his approval.

Jalynn stood. "You took the words out of my mouth, Dak. Let's go."

The Knox and Hansley kids followed Jalynn up the stairs to the game room. They chalked up pool cues, put on some music, and played several games of pool. They quickly became friends. Afton, the oldest of the Hansleys, was 17, the same age as Dakota. Ethan was 13, a year younger than Hank, and Evelyn was 11, a year older than Jalynn.

A couple of hours later, Dakota asked, "Would anyone like to go bodyboarding? The waves aren't very good for surfing today. But they look fun for bodyboarding."

"I'm in!" Jalynn said.

Afton looked a little nervous at the prospect. "I've never really—"

"I'd love to!" Ethan said, "We've never done it. Maybe you guys can show us how."

"For sure," Dakota said. "Bodyboarding is super easy and really fun."

Hank yawned. "I'm still stuffed from breakfast. I think I'll pass."

"No way, Hank—you're coming!" Ethan insisted.

After some debate, they all agreed to go. The Hansleys walked home, put on their swimsuits, and got some boards. A short time later, the six of them walked down the trail to the beach.

"So, you've never done this?" Dakota asked Afton.

"No. The water is pretty cold in England, and we're about an hour's drive from the beach."

"What do you like to do for fun?"

"I played volleyball all through high school. I like to run, read a good book, hang out with friends."

"That's cool."

"What about you?"

"I played lacrosse in high school. But for fun, I'd rather surf or snowboard or play my guitar."

"That all sounds fun. Bodyboarding sounds fun."

"Yeah. I think you're going to like it. And I saw in the news this morning that there have only been a couple of fatal shark attacks here this month. So I think we'll be fine."

"What?" Afton said. "Are you serious?"

"No. I'm just messin' with you," Dakota said, laughing.

Afton, who was walking behind him, kicked sand up on the back of his legs.

"Hey!"

Dakota gave the Hansleys some bodyboarding tips, and they all ran into the water.

After her third ride, Afton paddled back out to Dakota and said, "This is so fun! I rode that last wave all the way to the shore."

Dakota gave her a high five and said, "I saw! You have it down, girl!"

The six of them stayed in the water, catching waves, talking, and laughing for a couple of hours.

• • •

That evening, the Hansley's joined the Knoxes in their back-yard for dinner. William grilled **shish kabobs** on bamboo skewers. The smell of marinated steak and chicken, peppers, onions, and pineapple swirled around the backyard. The Hansleys brought a big bowl of fruit and rice.

Dakota and Afton sat down across from each other at the end of a table.

Afton said, "This food looks amazing."

"It does," Dakota said, "and I'm starving."

Afton said, "Thanks for showing us how to bodyboard today. I loved it."

"You're welcome."

"I never knew it was so fun."

Dakota smiled. "Wait 'til you try surfing."

"Surfing? Shouldn't I master bodyboarding first?"

Dakota shook his head. "Nah. We'll have you surfing by the end of summer."

"Wow. Okay!" Afton smiled.

"So," Dakota asked, "you live in London?"

"Yeah, in an area called Marylebone."

"Are you going to college in the fall?"

"Yes! The University of London," Afton said.

"That's probably close to your house."

"Yeah, close enough to ride my bike."

Dakota pulled off some vegetables from a skewer with his fork. "What are you going to major in?"

"Business management and administration."

"Wow."

"I wanted to major in history and be a schoolteacher teaching history, but my parents talked me out of that. So, for now, it's business management."

Nodding with a full mouth, Dakota finally said, "I love history, but business management sounds cool, too, Afton."

"How about you, Dakota. Are you going to college?"

"Yes, Liberty University in Virginia."

"Nice. What are you going to major in?"

"I want to study criminal justice and maybe work for our Department of Homeland Security."

"Really?"

Dakota nodded. "I love my country. And I want to help protect it."

"That's a noble career," Afton said. "I've never been to the United States."

"You should come sometime."

"I think I will. I know I'd like it. And you should come to

England!"

"I should!"

"I'll show you around."

"That would be fun."

Afton took a sip of her **strawberry lemonade**. "Hey, I heard our moms talking earlier, and apparently, we're all doing a tour of Israel, starting tomorrow."

"Oh!" Dakota was surprised. "I hadn't heard yet."

"Yeah, from what I understood, it sounded like it's going to be a 5-day guided tour of Israel."

"That's cool," Dakota said. "There are so many historical and archaeological sites to see here!"

"Yeah, I think it will be fascinat-  ing. They wanted to do a longer tour, but our dads start work on Monday."

As they continued talking, Dakota was mesmerized. He loved Afton's British accent, sense of humor, green eyes, smile, and thick, light brown hair. When the Hansleys left, Dakota was convinced he had just spent the evening talking with the prettiest girl he'd ever met. He walked upstairs to his room, opened his journal, and wrote: *Wow! What a fun day. I spent most of the day with my new friend and next-door neighbor here in Israel, Afton Hansley. She's amazing. I love her personality, and she's beautiful! But someone like that must have a boyfriend!*

66

Chapter 9
Wednesday, June 1, Herzliya.

The next morning, the Knoxes boarded the air-conditioned **tour bus**. Dakota quickly scanned the seating options. Afton was seated by a window on the driver's side of the bus. Right next to her on the center aisle was an empty seat. She looked up and smiled at Dakota as he walked down the aisle. He offered her a half-smile, turned, and sat down by a window three rows in front of her.

As they drove north, Dakota felt terrible. He had decided the night before not to sit next to Afton on the bus. But as he sat there by himself, he knew it was a bad decision. He had no one to talk to on the hour drive to Mount Carmel, and neither did Afton.

When the tour group arrived at their first stop, Afton walked over to Dakota in the parking lot and said, "Hey,

Dakota. Good morning. How are you doing?"

"I'm good. How are you?"

"Good. That was a pretty drive up the coast."

Dakota agreed. "Beautiful! Hey . . ." He was about to explain why he sat by himself, but Afton started to say something, so he said, "Ladies first."

Afton asked, "Did I say something last night that upset you?"

"Not at all. I really enjoyed talking to you last night. Why do you ask?"

"I don't know. You sat by yourself on the bus. I thought maybe I had accidentally said something rude or hurtful."

"Oh, I'm sorry. I'm not mad at all. I just wanted to give you some breathing room. I've heard some girls talk about how uncomfortable they've felt with guys who show them too much attention, too quickly. And honestly, I figured you must have a boyfriend back in England. And I thought, 'He wouldn't want me sitting—"

Afton chuckled. "Wow, okay, so I was way off—I'm sorry. I thought you were mad at me."

"Not in the slightest."

"Well, I'm relieved. I don't have a boyfriend. So you don't need to worry about that. And I wouldn't have thought you were showing me too much attention if you'd sat next to me on the bus. We're friends now, right? Next-door neighbors."

"Right. Neighbors. Friends."

Afton laughed. "Of course, you're my *only* friend here."

Dakota laughed. "Same."

As they walked to catch up to the tour group, Afton said, "You know I was pretty sad the first two days in Israel because all my friends are back in England. But after we met you guys and went bodyboarding yesterday, my mood totally changed. I thought, 'I'll have some friends here in Israel after all!' So thanks again for hanging out with us yesterday. And that was so nice of your parents to invite us over for dinner."

"Of course. We enjoyed hanging out with you guys, too."

• • •

Meanwhile, Ahmed and Eeman sat on **the beach** in front of their rental house in Herzliya.

Ahmed moved his chair to stay close to the shade of the umbrella. "Are you going out in the water, Eeman?"

"No. You know I can't swim."

Ahmed laughed.

Eeman shook his head. "At least I'm not afraid of sharks, like you!"

"Yeah, because you know you'll never see one sitting on the beach!"

"Very funny."

"Does Radomir know his bodyguard can't swim?"

Eeman started to respond, but Ahmed's phone rang.

"Hello."

"Hey Ahmed, it's Avner. Can you talk?"

"Sure. Where are you? Why are you whispering?"

"I'm in my office at the museum. I don't want anyone to hear me. What are you up to?"

"Eeman and I are sitting on the beach getting skin cancer."

"That's nice," Avner said. "Hey, I have great news on two fronts."

Since Radomir's first phone call to Avner on May 14, Ahmed and Avner had had several conversations about the details of the heist. They had mapped out the path Avner would take through the museum when the power went out. They decided what time the drone would arrive and other details. But there were still two big wrinkles to iron out before the heist could go down.

Avner told Ahmed, "The first bit of good news is: I got the code to the vault!"

"Sweet! How'd you get it?"

"My dad had it on his phone. He finally left his phone in a place where I could look at it for a few minutes. I went into his Notes app. And there it was. So I came into work early this morning and tested it out. And it worked! The vault opened. I was able to locate the Isaiah Scroll. It's long and flat. I'll have to roll it up, but—"

"Hold on. You opened the vault?"

"Yeah, I wanted to test it ahead of—"

"I understand that, but you know the camera recorded that."

"For sure it did," Avner said. "But we're taking out the data center, right? And they don't check the videos unless there's a theft. So unless a theft takes place before ours, we should be fine."

"Okay, cool. Good work, Avner. Geneviève is going to be so happy!"

Eeman shook his head and laughed. "Oh, that is so cruel!"

"What did Eeman say?" Avner asked.

Ahmed motioned to Eeman to be quiet and told Avner, "Oh, a guy had a great ride on a wave, and Eeman said, 'That is so *cool*.'"

"Ahh, okay. I have more good news," Avner said. "Our nighttime security guard dilemma is solved. Long story, but Gershom, a close friend and coworker, is going to misdirect the guards on the night of the heist while I collect the artifacts."

"You're brought another guy in on this?"

"We need his help, Ahmed."

"You should have run this by me first. You trust this guy, Gershom?"

"For sure," Avner said. "He really needs the money, and I promised him a good size cut if we pull it off."

"*If* we pull it off?" Ahmed said. "No. *When* we pull it off."

"You're right," Avner said. "*When* we pull it off. Hey, is Geneviève back from her trip to Mongolia? I'm looking forward to finally meeting her."

"No, man, she's still off the grid with no Internet or phone. Long vacation."

"Hmm. She told me it was a work trip."

"Yeah, uh, it's like a working vacation for her."

"Well, if you talk to her, tell her I said, 'Hello,'" Avner said. "Absolutely!"

"Got to go. Someone knocked on my door."

Chapter 10
Saturday, June 4, Masada, Israel.

The Knoxes and Hansleys' tour guide Benjamin Melamed greeted the tour group at the base of **Masada**. "Good morning, everyone. Today's the fourth day of our five-day tour, and we've got a wonderful day planned for you. We're beginning the day by taking a cable car to the top of this massive plateau overlooking the Dead Sea. Follow me, and I'll tell you more about it when we get to the top."

Dakota raised his hand. "Excuse me, Benjamin, I heard there's a trail people can hike to get up to the top. How long does that take to walk?"

Benjamin said, "Yes, it's called **Snake Trail**. And you *could* hike it. It would take a strong, healthy guy like you about 45 minutes. So, you'd miss a bit of the tour at the top. And I must warn you. After the sun comes up in the summer, the trail gets hot. I'd advise against it."

Jalynn whispered to Afton, "Dakota's afraid of heights. Not flying, mainly just dangly things like gondolas and cable cars. Hates them!"

"Oh, I didn't know that," Afton said.

"I heard that, Jay," Dakota said.

Afton looked at Dakota. "I didn't know strong, healthy guys were afraid of cable cars." She walked off with the tour group, then turned around and said, "Come on. You got this!"

As Dakota followed her onto the cable car, he tried to explain. "I only feel a *little* uncomfortable on things like this."

"Oh, of course."

After the door shut and the **cable car** began to move, Dakota whispered to Afton, "Whenever I'm on these things, I just imagine what would happen if the cable snapped or slid off, and how we'd go tumbling end over end, down the cliff, and hit those jagged rocks, and we'd—"

"Okay, stop. We're going to be fine."

"You're right. Sorry."

Halfway to the top, as everyone except Dakota was marveling about the view, the cable car came to an abrupt stop and started swinging gently from front to back.

Dakota looked at Afton. "Hmm? I told you these things are sketch—"

Afton laughed. "Relax."

"Next time, you and I are *walking* up!"

"Next time? Are we coming back here?"

"Probably not. But *if* we ever do."

"Like years from now, *ever*?" Afton asked.

"Yeah, you know, if we're still friends and we—"

"*If* we're still friends?"

"I meant, *when* we're still friends and *if* we . . . Actually, I should be quiet. I'm a little nervous."

Afton smiled. "I'm just playin' with you."

Their tour guide said, "I'm sure we'll be moving again soon. While we're waiting, I'll point out that Herod the Great had a palace built near the top of this plateau around 30 BC. We'll see the ruins of it here shortly. Of course, the Bible tells us that Herod was the king in Israel at the time of Jesus's birth. He was the one who tried to have Jesus killed after He was born. The first-century historian Flavius Josephus spoke about him. And a wealth of archaeological evidence has confirmed his existence. Discoveries include a piece of a wine jug dating back to 19 BC uncovered here at Masada. The Latin inscription on the jug includes a reference to Herod and his title, "Herod, king of Judea."

Dakota remembered learning about this discovery and seeing a photograph of the wine jug inscription.

Benjamin continued. "Other discoveries related to Herod include **coins with Herod's name on them** and the ruins of his hilltop palace south of Jerusalem known as the Herodium. These discoveries support the New Testament accounts and leave no doubt that Herod was a historical figure who reigned in the very position described in the Gospels."

The cable car started to move.

Dakota breathed a sigh of relief and whispered, "Thank

God!" He turned to Afton and said, "I'm going to stand by the door."

Jalynn told Afton, "He wants to be the first one to get off."

Afton smiled and gave Jalynn a side hug. "I love your play-by-play commentary Jalynn! Thank you."

"He's my big brother—I could tell you all *kinds* of things about him."

"Mostly good, I'm sure?"

"Hmm . . . mostly."

After an hour exploring the ruins of Herod's fortress, Benjamin announced that they'd be boarding the cable car and heading back to the bus in 20 minutes. Dakota turned to Afton, "I'm going to run down the hill."

"Seriously?"

"Yeah. It's all downhill . . . will only take about 15 minutes."

"Cuz you don't like the cable car?"

"Well, that's a *tiny* part of it, but—"

Afton looked at him as if to say, "Really?"

He laughed. "All right, it's a *big* part of it! But I also think it will be fun. Want to come?"

"Okay. Why not?"

Snake Trail, Masada

They let their parents know and took off jogging down the trail. It was hot, but it was downhill the whole way. So they skipped, jumped, and said 'hello' to people they passed. Fifteen minutes later, they were at the bottom.

"We did it!" Dakota said.

Afton laughed. "I haven't run down a trail like that since I was a kid. That was fun."

"Yeah, it's good to be a kid again! You can't experience Masada like that in a cable car."

A couple of minutes later, the tour group arrived. After boarding the bus, they drove north and hiked to the waterfall oasis at En Gedi. The next stop was **Qumran**, to see **where the Dead Sea Scrolls were discovered**. The group finished the day by floating in the salty water of the Dead Sea.

On the long bus ride back to Herzliya, Dakota looked out the window and reflected on the past few days. Afton was asleep against the window to his left. As he thought of all the fun they had, he couldn't help but wonder about the possibility

Qumran

of a relationship with her. They had just spent ten hours a day together for the past four days, and he loved everything about her. *She's a Christian. She's smart. She's fun to hang out with, beautiful, humble, funny, and not afraid of a little adventure.*

Dakota thought ahead to the last day of summer when they would have to part ways. The thought of having to say "so long" to her brought a tear to his eye. As he pondered that sad fact, the bus went around a long curve. Afton slowly fell over to her right until her head rested on Dakota's left shoulder. He let her rest there, but that brought another tear to his eye, and that one ran down his cheek. He thought *I don't want to say 'goodbye' to this girl. But how can I even think about being with a girl who lives on the other side of the planet? It wouldn't work. And I've never even had a girlfriend. How would I tell her how I feel? I don't know. But I think she's amazing. God, please lead me. Grant me wisdom, and may Your will be done.*

Dakota's mom got up from her seat to get something from the overhead bin. She saw Afton sleeping on Dakota's shoulder and smiled as if to say, "Isn't that *so* sweet!" Then she saw Dakota's wet cheek. She mouthed, "Are you okay?"

Dakota nodded, yes.

Abigail mouthed, "She's *so* cute."

Not wanting to wake her up, Dakota gave a tiny nod in agreement.

A few minutes later, the bus hit some bumps in the road. Afton stirred and realized she was sleeping on Dakota's shoulder. "Oh my gosh! I'm so sorry."

"No need to apologize," Dakota said. "It's been a long day. I didn't want to wake you."

"How long was I leaning on your shoulder?"

"Maybe 20 minutes."

"Oh, my goodness. I'm embarrassed."

"Please don't be."

When the families got off the bus in Herzliya, Dakota asked Benjamin, "What do you have scheduled for us tomorrow?"

"We're going to start the day at the Israel Museum in Jerusalem."

"Awesome. That's where the Dead Sea Scrolls are housed."

"Yes! And lots of other archaeological discoveries."

"Thanks, Benjamin, for a great day today. Tomorrow will be a blast!"

Chapter 11
Sunday, June 5, Israel Museum, Jerusalem.

The tour of the Israel Museum the following day didn't include a ride on the tour bus. So the Knoxes and Hansleys hopped into their cars to make the 48-mile drive to Jerusalem. Dakota's parents decided to drive the red Bronco. They gave Dakota permission to drive the gray one and bring whoever would like to go with him. Tagging along with Dakota was an easy decision for Hank and Ethan Hansley. They jumped into the back seat.

As Dakota was familiarizing himself with the controls, Afton opened the passenger door. "Mind if I drive with you guys?"

Dakota smiled. "Of course not. Hop in." As they drove off, Dakota said, "Wasn't En Gedi amazing yesterday? I loved seeing where David sought refuge from Saul in the Old Testament."

"Yes, and that waterfall! The whole day was incredible."

"But no more hiking or sketchy cable cars today," Dakota said. "We're on the ground, riding in style!"

When they arrived at the Israel Museum, they joined their families outside the main entrance where their guide Benjamin was waiting.

"All right, folks, good morning! What a beautiful day," Benjamin said. "It's great to see you all on the final day of the tour. Follow me. We're going to start in the archaeological wing."

"Benjamin's been a fantastic tour guide," Dakota said to Afton.

Afton agreed. "He's so knowledgeable about Israel's history and archaeology. I heard him say he's led more than 100 tours."

About an hour into the museum tour, they came to the "Tel Dan Stele," more popularly known as "the David Inscription."

Benjamin said, "As I mentioned yesterday at En Gedi, David was the king of Israel for 40 years, from about 1011–971 BC. Of course, he's known for his deep love for God, writing many of the Psalms, and being an ancestor of Jesus. Up until 1993, the evidence for David's life was limited to the Bible and Flavius Josephus. So, it had become fashionable in some academic circles to dismiss the David stories as mere invention. Philip Davies, a former professor at the University of Sheffield in England, said 'King David is about as historical as King Arthur.'"

"That's ridiculous," Dakota muttered.

Benjamin went on explaining. "The critics' verdict was that David was nothing more than a figure of religious and political mythology. Well, their assaults on David were dealt a major setback in 1993 when this nearly 3000-year-old stone slab was discovered in the ruins at Dan in northern Israel. The Aramaic inscription on the **slab mentions 'the king of Israel' and the 'king of the House of David.'** This was an amazing discovery! It helped to verify for the first time in a contemporary text outside the Bible that David was a real historical figure. In light of this discovery, *Time* magazine rightly acknowledged: 'The skeptics' claim that King David never existed is now hard to defend.'"

Afton looked at Dakota. "Another discovery that mentions a person in the Bible. Amazing!"

"Isn't it? A guy named Charlie Campbell came to our church about a year ago and gave a presentation on archaeological discoveries that have verified details in the Bible. So I'm familiar with this discovery. But it's awesome to see it with my own eyes."

A while later, the tour group walked into the "Jesus of Nazareth" section of the museum. Benjamin said, "New Testament writers tell us that Pontius Pilate was the Roman governor of Judea who oversaw Jesus's trial and then sentenced Him to death by crucifixion. Was Pilate a legendary figure?"

"Nope!" Hank exclaimed.

"You're right!" Benjamin said. "Flavius Josephus wrote

about him. A Jewish philosopher, Philo of Alexandria, mentioned him, as did the Roman historian Tacitus. But archaeologists have also verified his existence. In 1961, archaeologists were digging in Caesarea, on the beautiful coast of the Mediterranean Sea here in Israel."

Afton whispered to Dakota, "Isn't Caesarea right up the coast from Herzliya?"

"Yes!"

"We should go sometime!"

"For sure!"

Benjamin continued explaining the discovery. "While clearing away the sand and overgrowth from the jumbled ruins of an ancient Roman theater, they unearthed this **limestone block** with a first-century Latin **inscription that mentioned 'Pontius Pilate, Prefect of Judea.'**"

Dakota and Afton stepped forward a few steps to get a better look at the inscription.

Benjamin pointed and said, "This inscription confirmed that Pontius Pilate was a real person and that he had the authority, as prefect, to condemn or pardon Jesus, just as the Gospel accounts report."

"What a great discovery!" Dakota said to Afton. "I love this stuff."

She agreed.

Benjamin pointed to

a stone box, about 30 inches long, to the left of the Pontius Pilate inscription. "We believe this stone box, called an ossuary, held the bones of another person you've read about in the New Testament. The Gospel writers tell us

that a man named Caiaphas was the Jewish high priest at the time of Jesus. He presided over the late-night trial where Jesus acknowledged He was the Messiah. Might Caiaphas have been a New Testament fabrication?"

Hank raised his hand. "That would be another 'No,' Ben."

"Good answer, Hank. Caiaphas was not an invention. Flavius Josephus mentioned him. And archaeology has helped to confirm his existence. In 1990, construction workers accidentally unearthed a first-century Jewish burial cave about two miles south of Jerusalem."

Dakota told Afton, "They can hardly dig anywhere over here without finding something of significance."

"It sure seems that way," she said.

"Because of its enormous weight," Benjamin explained, "a bulldozer unintentionally broke through the roof of the cave. Inside were several stone bone boxes, including this uncharacteristically ornate one. Inside it were the bones of a man who was approximately sixty years old at the time of his death. On the outside of the **ossuary, inscribed in Aramaic, is the name Joseph, son of Caiaphas**. You can see it here."

Several people in the group stepped forward to look at the inscription.

Afton's dad Steven raised his hand for clarification. "I thought the high priest's name was just Caiaphas."

Benjamin replied, "Although the Gospel writers and Flavius Josephus referred to the high priest as Caiaphas, Josephus tells us that the priest's full name was Joseph Caiaphas—the very name etched into the side of the ossuary."

"Interesting. Okay, thank you."

"You're quite welcome," Benjamin said. "And close by Caiaphas's ossuary is another artifact I'd like to point out. Over here, we have evidence that the Romans crucified people in the first century. As you all know, the Bible indicates that Jesus was crucified with nails. But critics of the Bible said crucifixions with nails didn't take place in Israel in the first century. Why? No material evidence of any crucified victim had ever been uncovered in the holy land. So, scholars dismissed the Gospels' accounts as either imagined or inaccurate. They argued that nails could not have been used to fasten a crucified victim to a cross because the anatomy of hands and feet could not support the weight of a body. Well, critics of the Gospels were shown to be wrong when a construction crew accidentally discovered an ancient Jewish cemetery in Jerusalem. It contained the remains of several men who were killed during the Jewish revolt against Rome around AD 70. One of the bone ossuaries contained the skeleton of a young man who had been put to death by crucifixion with nails."

"How was that determined?" someone in the tour group asked.

Benjamin said, "He still had an iron spike driven through

his heel bone. You can see it right here. Notice the **heel bone with the spike** through it."

"Whoa!" Afton said.

"Isn't that crazy?" Dakota remarked.

Benjamin pointed at the spike and said, "The head of the spike is here on the left, and the bent tip is on the right. The Romans typically removed the nails from their victims because iron was expensive. But apparently, this nail was too difficult to remove. The tip of the nail had been bent back toward the head, likely the result of hitting a knot in the wood. So the Roman soldiers left it there. And now, 2,000 years later, we have solid archaeological evidence that the Romans *did* crucify people *in* Israel, *in* the first century, with *nails*, just like the Bible says."

When Benjamin finished his sentence, Dakota heard someone behind him mutter, "Not for long."

Not for long? What does that mean? Dakota turned around to see who had said that. A few feet behind him was a young man, about 25 years old and five feet, nine inches tall.

He had straight black hair pulled back in a ponytail and a thin black beard. He was wearing khaki-colored chino pants and a navy-blue sports coat and tie. On his jacket was a name badge. He appeared to be part of the museum's staff.

He was startled when Dakota turned around and quickly walked away.

Thoughts raced through Dakota's mind. *Was the guy implying that something bad was going to happen to the artifacts? Maybe I misheard him. Perhaps he was saying that our museum tour wasn't going to go on much longer.* Dakota wasn't sure, but he was able to remember the man's name—it was on his name badge: Avner.

"Okay, everyone," Benjamin said, "we've spent three hours in the archaeological wing of the museum. We could spend a couple of days here, but let's head over to the Shrine of the Book, the building that houses the Dead Sea Scrolls."

The tour group followed Benjamin outside. As they walked, Benjamin said, "Some critics of the Bible say that the Bible has been translated and copied so many times down through the centuries, we can't trust what it says today."

"A friend of mine in London thinks that!" Afton told Dakota.

"Yeah," Dakota said, "it's a popular claim, but it's a mistaken one. And the ancient manuscript copies of the Bible reveal that to be the case. That's probably what Benjamin is about to talk about."

"In 1947," Benjamin said, "a twelve-year-old Arab boy made one of the greatest archaeological discoveries of all time. While looking for a lost goat in Qumran, near the Dead Sea, he threw a stone into a cave and heard the sound of shattering pottery."

Dakota whispered to Afton, "You don't even need to be a professional archaeologist to find things in Israel."

Afton nodded her head.

"The boy was curious about the noise," Benjamin said. "So he entered the cave and found a collection of **large clay jars**

containing carefully wrapped leather manuscripts. What this boy stumbled upon was an ancient collection of handwritten copies of the Old Testament that dated as far back as the third century BC."

Afton looked at Dakota. "From *before* Jesus? That's so cool!"

Benjamin continued talking. "Archaeologists spent years searching the surrounding caves. By the time they were done, some 220 copies of Old Testament books had been found. These included nineteen copies of the Book of Isaiah, twenty-five copies of Deuteronomy, and thirty copies of the Psalms. When the search ended, the only Old Testament book that wasn't found was a copy of the Book of Esther."

Dakota raised his hand. "Benjamin, do they know why they didn't have a copy of the Book of Esther?"

"Well, the Book of Esther is actually mentioned in some of the other Dead Sea Scrolls. So we know the Jews at Qumran were familiar with it and probably had it."

Afton asked, "How was it determined that the scrolls dated back to the time before Christ?"

"Well," Benjamin said, "one indication the scrolls were from that period was the coins archaeologists discovered alongside the scrolls. They found several hundred coins with the scrolls that were minted between 135 BC and AD 68. And more recently, a new, improved method of carbon-14 dating also determined the scrolls belonged to that time. So there are

no doubts about their antiquity."

Afton nodded. "Thank you."

Benjamin led them into the **Shrine of the Book**. "The corridor leading into the Shrine resembles a cave, recalling the site where the ancient manuscripts were discovered. The white-domed roof you saw outside was designed to look like the lids of the jars that the first scrolls were found in."

As Benjamin continued explaining the history of the building, Dakota noticed that Avner was in the Shrine of the Book. *There's the guy who mumbled that troubling comment ten minutes ago. Why is he over here now? Is he following our group?* Dakota kept an eye on him.

Benjamin continued talking. "Many of the Dead Sea Scrolls are housed here in this building in a climate-controlled vault. But, as you can see, there are several on display here. These scrolls and thousands of other manuscripts dating back to the time of the early church have allowed Biblical scholars and textual experts to recover the text of the Bible that Christians used 2,000 years ago. We can be confident that the text of the Bible we use today is very accurate to the originals penned by the Biblical writers."

Benjamin encouraged them to walk around and look at the manuscripts.

Dakota nudged Afton. "Let's go look at this one over here where it's less crowded."

"Okay."

They turned and headed to an exhibit on the wall. As they looked at the ancient manuscript, Dakota angled his body to keep an eye on Avner. He whispered, "Afton, I need to tell you something."

"What is it?"

"Don't look now, but there's a guy over there in a navy sports coat with black hair. He works here. He was standing behind us earlier and muttered something strange. Benjamin was talking about how these archaeological artifacts verify details in the Bible, and I heard the guy mumble, 'Not for long.'"

"Really?" Afton asked, "What do you think he meant?"

"I don't know for sure. He walked off when he realized I heard him. But then, he followed our group into this room. I'm wondering if he's up to something."

"Maybe you should report it to one of the security guards."

"I think I should."

"There's a security guard right there."

"Come with me?"

"Of course."

Dakota approached the security guard. "Excuse me. Hi. Could you please direct me to the security office? I'd like to report something suspicious."

"Sure. What is it?"

"I'd rather talk to whoever's in charge."

"Okay. Suit yourself." He pointed and told Dakota where to go.

"Thank you."

When Dakota and Afton got to the security office, Dakota asked the woman behind the glass, "Can we speak to the head of security, please? We'd like to report something."

"He's very busy. May I ask what it . . . Oh! He's walking by right now." Spinning her chair toward him, she said, "Mr. Haddad, this young man and his friend would like to report something."

He smiled at them and said, "Why don't you step into my office."

As they followed him in, Dakota noticed a sign on the door: *Chief Security and Contingency Officer*. After they sat down, Dakota explained to him what Avner had said.

Mr. Haddad, a man in his late sixties, said, "I can sort of see why you'd be concerned. But it's likely you misunderstood him. I assure you, Avner is one of our most trusted employees. It's unlikely he would want to harm the artifacts in any way. But I'm writing this down, and if anything happens, I will make sure he's the first to be questioned."

Mr. Haddad finished writing some notes, stood, and thanked Dakota and Afton for stopping by.

"Thank you," Dakota said. "It was nice meeting you."

As they walked out into the warm summer heat, Dakota said, "Okay. I feel better."

"Yeah, it was good to let him know," Afton said. "What's the saying? 'If you see something, *say* something?' And you did."

"Thanks for coming with me, Afton. Let's find our families. They're probably still looking at the Dead Sea Scrolls. Did you happen to get the name of that security chief?"

"I did! I took one of his business cards." She reached into the front pocket of her denim shorts and pulled it out. "It says Chief Security and Contingency Officer, Gershom Haddad."

Chapter 12
Monday, June 6, Herzliya.

The following day, William Knox and Steven Hansley headed off to their first day at Light Shield Defense Systems.

Dakota was happy to sleep in and have nothing to do. When he rolled out of bed around 10:00 a.m., he looked out his window. *What a beautiful day! It feels like the first real day of summer—no homework to think about, no flight to catch, no touring. Nothing!*

He walked downstairs in his swim trunks, tank top, and flip-flops. He toasted a bagel and cut up a few strawberries and a banana. When his coffee was ready, he walked onto the deck to eat, read his Bible, and watch the waves. *Whoa—the waves look so fun!* When he finished eating, he thought, *I should go surf!*

As he waxed his surfboard, he noticed Afton was sitting outside her bedroom on the deck overlooking the Hansleys' backyard.

"Good morning, Afton!"

"Hey! Good morning, Dakota. Going surfing?"

"Yeah, the waves look fun! Want to go?"

"It looks so nice out there. Bodyboarding again would be fun."

"I'll teach you how to surf."

"No, I'd rather you have fun."

"It would be fun to teach you how to surf. And there's a longboard here that's perfect to learn on."

"Okay. That's sweet of you."

"Grab a towel and whatever you need. I'll wax the board."

After some instruction on the beach and a few wipeouts in the water, Dakota was confident Afton was on the cusp of success. When the next wave came, he turned her and the board toward the shore. Afton paddled, and Dakota guided her into the rolling swell with a gentle push.

"You got it this time!" Dakota said. And she did. She stood to her feet and angled the board toward the shore.

Dakota threw his hands in the air and yelled, "Go, girl! Yeah!"

She raced across the water for about 75 yards. When she hopped off the board, she turned around with a huge smile and started laughing.

Dakota walked through the water, splashing it with his hands to celebrate the accomplishment. "You did it! That was awesome. I'm so proud of you."

"That was one of the biggest thrills I've ever experienced," Afton said. "Thank you for your instruction and patience."

"You're welcome. Want to catch more?"

"I'd love to!"

Dakota helped guide her into a couple more waves. She stood to her feet each time.

"Now that you have the hang of it," Dakota said, "I'll go grab my board." He walked in, picked up his board, and paddled out. They caught waves, laughed, and told stories about their childhoods for the next hour and a half.

• • •

When Dakota and Afton returned to the Knoxes' house, their siblings were swimming in the pool.

"Hey, you two," Abigail said. "Looked like you were having a lot of fun out there. You learned how to surf, Afton! I saw you. You were amazing!"

"Well, your son's a wonderful teacher."

"You both must be starving. There are turkey sandwiches on the counter."

"Thanks, Mom!"

Dakota and Afton sat down by the pool to enjoy their lunch.

"Maybe tomorrow," Dakota said, "we, and whoever wants to go, can drive up the coast and explore that ancient theater in Caesarea."

"Where they found the Pontius Pilate inscription?"

"Yeah."

"It's not far. We should go see it!"

Abigail walked over. "Dakota, Mrs. Hansley and I talked. Our families are going to have dinner together tonight. Would you mind barbecuing hamburgers later?"

"Nope, I can do that."

"Thanks! I'd love for your father to relax when he gets home from work."

"Happy to help, Mom."

• • •

That evening at dinner, both dads agreed that it had been an enjoyable and fruitful day at Light Shield.

During dessert, Dakota got everyone's attention. "Tomorrow morning, Afton and I are driving up the coast to Caesarea. We're going to explore the ruins of the theater where the Pontius Pilate inscription was found. Let us know if you'd like to come."

"Not going," Jalynn said. "Toured out. I'd rather stay here and swim."

Hank raised his hand. "I second that."

The same was true for the other Hansley kids.

Dakota looked at Afton across the table. "Well, I guess it's just us."

"All right."

That night Afton texted Dakota:

> There's a coffee shop down by the marina that I found before you guys arrived. I'm going to ride my bike there tomorrow morning and get coffee for our drive to Caesarea. Would you like anything?

Dakota: That's nice of you. Seeing that I taught you how to surf, maybe you can teach me how to hold two hot coffees and ride a bike at the same time.

Afton: LOL. My bike has a cup holder on it, and I'll hold the other one in my hand. Not a problem.

Dakota: Or I'll just ride down there with you. Why don't I do that?

Afton: That would be even better :)

Dakota: What time?

Afton: How about 8:30?

Dakota: Perfect!

Chapter 13
Tuesday morning, June 7, Herzliya.

There wasn't a cloud in the sky as Dakota and Afton pedaled their beach cruisers to the coffee shop. When they arrived, Dakota looked up at the sign. "It's called 'Café Café'?"

"Yeah."

"I wonder how they came up with such a creative name."

"Funny. You're going to like it. Promise."

"We'll see." He pulled the door open for Afton. "I'm a little skeptical with that name. Where are we getting lunch later? Diner Diner?"

"Oh, you're on a roll, Dakota."

"And I haven't even had caffeine. Maybe on the way to Caesarea, we can listen to Duran Duran."

"Okay, stop," Afton said, chuckling.

When they walked out with their drinks, Dakota said, "Okay. I repent. You were right. This *is* good coffee! And their food looked amazing, too. And what a great location right here at the marina."

"My thoughts exactly," Afton said.

"Why don't we walk around for a minute. I haven't been down here yet."

"Sure," Afton said. "I'll lock the bikes."

As they walked down one of the docks, Dakota said, "I can't believe how many boats are here. There's hundreds. Some of these yachts are huge. Look at that one!"

"Amazing," Afton said. "Wouldn't it be fun to own one of these, and we . . . I mean you, you could sail around the world. Think of the waves you'd discover, Dakota!"

"I'd love that."

An older man stepped off what looked like the largest yacht in the marina. As he walked toward Dakota and Afton talking on his phone, a small gust of wind blew his hat off and into the water. Dakota ran down the dock about 20 yards, reached into the water, and retrieved it. He brushed off some of the water and handed it to the man.

"You're not supposed to be out here on the dock unless you're a boat owner," the man snarled.

"Whoa, my friend. Don't go overboard with the gratitude," Dakota said.

Afton bit her lip to keep from laughing at Dakota's sarcasm. She said, "Sir, we're sorry. We didn't know we weren't allowed to walk on the dock. We will happily turn around."

"Well, I do appreciate you grabbing my hat. These gray Homburgs are hard to find. But, yes, run along now."

Dakota and Afton turned around and walked back toward their bikes.

"That guy was a grump," Dakota said.

"Total Scrooge. That was nice of you to grab his hat before it sank or floated out of reach."

"Thanks."

"He was a Brit."

"Yeah, he *was* a brat," Dakota agreed.

"No, I said *Brit*—he was British. Not just his accent, but I overheard him say on his phone call that he was flying back to England soon. Whatever! Forget him. Let's go check out Caesarea!"

Back at the Knoxes' house, they sat down in the red Bronco. Dakota was about to push the Start button, but he stopped, looked over at Afton, and smiled. "I have an idea."

"What's that?"

"I just remembered the tops on these Broncos can be lifted off to give them a convertible type of feel. The weather is so nice; it seems like the perfect day to try it!"

"I'd love to! I've never driven in a convertible."

They got out and removed all three sections of the black top.

A few minutes later, they were driving up the coast, soaking up the coastal sunshine, singing along to a song.

"I love the open air, but I should have brought a hat," Afton said, laughing.

Dakota glanced over at her. Afton's thick light brown hair that usually hung a couple of inches below her shoulders was blowing all over the place. "I've got you covered." He reached into the back seat and grabbed his brown and yellow San

Diego Padres hat. "How about this?"

"Perfect! Thanks."

She looked at the hat and put it on. She had no idea what the "SD" on the cap stood for, so she decided it would stand for "Sweet Dakota."

When they arrived at Caesarea, Dakota parked the Bronco in the dirt by the **ancient Roman theater**. As they walked up the theater's stone steps, Afton said, "What a beautiful view of the ocean the people would have had from these seats!"

Dakota agreed. "And you can see the remains of Herod the Great's seaside palace right there."

"Wow! That's where he lived?"

"Yeah, when he was in Caesarea. But he had several palaces that archaeologists have identified, like the one we saw at Masada. But this is the theater where his grandson Herod Agrippa was hailed as a god in Acts, chapter 12."

"Really?"

Dakota nodded, "Yes, and Flavius Josephus verifies that in his book, *Antiquities of the Jews*."

"Wow!"

"He even verifies that Agrippa died a short time later, just

as Luke reported."

After looking at the theater, they walked toward the water to look at the ruins of Herod's palace.

Dakota said, "When the apostle Paul was imprisoned here at Caesarea, he may have been held right here in the palace structure. We don't know for sure. But Paul *did* have hearings here before Felix and Festus, Roman governors, in Acts 24 through 26. They lived here after Herod died."

"How do you know all this interesting stuff?" Afton asked.

"On our long flight from San Diego, I read a book on Biblical archaeology. It had more than a hundred photos of discoveries that verify details in the Bible."

"Oh, wow. What's the book called?"

"*Archaeological Evidence for the Bible.*"

"I'll have to get a copy."

"You can have mine. I finished it."

They walked north a couple of hundred yards, where Dakota pointed out the ruins of Herod's man-made harbor. "This is the harbor that Luke says Paul sailed out of and returned to."

"Right here? That's amazing," Afton said. "I need to reread the Book of Acts."

"That book about archaeology mentioned that more than eighty details in the Book of Acts have been confirmed by historical and archaeological research."

"Whoa!'

"When we read the Bible, we're not reading about mythological people. We're reading about real people. Josephus writes about more than a dozen people mentioned in the New Testament, including Herod the Great, Pontius Pilate, John the Baptist, Caiaphas, and even Jesus!"

"That's mind-blowing, Dakota!"

"Hey! Look at that. They rent **stand-up paddleboards**. Why don't we rent a couple and check out the ruins of the harbor from the water!"

"That would be amazing! I've never been on a stand-up board, but it can't be any harder than surfing. Right?"

"Exactly! It's *way* easier. Let's do it!"

• • •

After exploring the harbor and some other ruins at Caesarea, they strolled back toward the Bronco. As they talked about favorite bands and foods, Afton wondered if their friendship was turning into something more. *I definitely like him. He's kind, intelligent, funny, adventuresome, handsome—I love how tall he is and his light brown hair and blue eyes—but what I like most of all is that he loves Jesus. But he lives so far away. How could a relationship work? We could FaceTime. I don't know. My heart aches at the thought that our time together will end when summer is over.*

• • •

Later that evening at the Knoxes' house, Dakota and Afton told some of the kids what they had seen at Caesarea.

"We stood in the theater where Herod Agrippa was struck with worms in Acts 12," Dakota said. "It's still there. You guys should have come."

"I hate worms," Hank said.

Dakota laughed.

Abigail walked over to Dakota with a jar in her hand. "All right, Indy. Help me open this. I can't get it."

Afton looked perplexed. "Indy? Is that a nickname?"

"No," Dakota said. "She was making a reference to Indiana Jones."

"Oh."

"You've seen the movie. Right?"

"No, but I've heard—"

"You haven't seen Indiana Jones with Harrison Ford?"

Afton cringed. "No."

"Well, you have to watch it, at least the first one!"

"What's it about?"

"Well, Indiana Jones, an archaeologist, is hired by the U.S. government to find the ark of the covenant, the gold-covered chest that the Israelites carried the Ten Commandments in. But Adolf Hitler's Nazis are looking for it at the same time. It's a fun movie."

Jalynn pointed a finger in the air, spun around, and said, "Movie night at the Knox house!"

"Hold on," Abigail said. "Isn't there some bad language and inappropriate content?"

"It's PG, Mom," Dakota said. "And the filter we subscribe to takes those parts out."

"Ah, yes, I forgot that. I'll check with Nicola to make sure she and Steven are okay with the Hansley kids watching it."

Jalynn opened the pantry. "I'll make the popcorn. Afton, you're sitting next to me, and we can close our eyes during the scary parts."

"Sounds good, Jalynn!" Afton lowered her voice and told Dakota, "Your sister is so cute!"

The kids made their way down the hall to the movie-viewing room. The room had a large built-in screen and eight black leather recliners.

Ethan Hansley plopped down in the front row. "These seats are awesome! Blue LED lights around the rim of the cup holders? Nice."

"Yeah. And check out this button," Hank said. "You can recline and put your legs up."

After the popcorn and drinks were passed out, Dakota and Afton sat with Jalynn and Evelyn in the back row, and Hank hit play.

When the movie was over, Afton turned to Dakota in his seat. "I really liked the movie, Dakota. Thank you."

"I thought you would."

"I can't believe I never saw it. But you know what I've liked even more?"

"What?"

"Seeing real artifacts here in Israel."

"For sure."

"The movie does make me wonder if the Ark of the Covenant is out there somewhere, Dakota. Do you think it is?"

"It might be. But archaeologists don't know where."

"Hmm . . . maybe they'll find it someday."

"Maybe."

"Well, it's late. I should get my brother and sister home."

"I'll walk you guys back."

As Dakota walked with the Hansleys, Ethan looked at him and said, "You don't have to walk us home."

Afton objected. "It's very kind of him to walk us home and make sure we make it safely."

"This neighborhood is totally safe!" Ethan shot back. When they reached the Hansley's house, he said, "I loved the movie, Dakota! Thanks for showing it to us."

After Ethan and Evelyn walked inside, Afton said, "Thank you for a great day, Dakota. The past two days have been *so* fun. Actually, this whole time in Israel has been amazing."

"You're welcome. I agree. It's been so fun. All right, sleep well, Afton. We'll see you guys tomorrow."

She smiled. "Goodnight, Dakota."

Afton slowly walked up the stairs to her bedroom and thought, *These last few days have been some of the best days of my life. Thank You, God, for Israel. Thank You for Dakota. I love that guy. He is so sweet, so fun, so cute . . . and He loves You!*

She walked on the deck outside her bedroom. She leaned on the rail and looked west over the moonlit Mediterranean Sea. She felt a slight ocean breeze on her face and continued praying. *God, might Dakota be the person I've been waiting for and praying about since I was little? I don't know. He's the kind of guy I've always wanted to be with. But You know what's best. I will trust You. Guide us, Father, according to Your will. In Jesus's name, I pray. Amen.*

As Afton turned to walk inside, she glanced over at the Knoxes' house. Dakota was plucking the strings of his acoustic guitar by the fire in his backyard. She stepped inside, slid the door shut, and opened a window. *Falling asleep to the beautiful melodies he's playing feels like the perfect way to end an amazing day—goodnight, sweet Dakota.*

Chapter 14
Tuesday, June 7, Jerusalem.

On the same morning that Dakota and Afton rode their bikes to the marina for coffee, Avner woke up, checked his phone, and saw a text from Ahmed:

Looking forward to the party tonight.

That was code for saying that everything was on schedule for the heist later that night. Avner smiled and messaged him back:

Yes, looking forward to it!

Avner showered, grabbed a muffin, and walked out the front door of his parents' house. The plan he and Ahmed had come up with required that he walk to work, something he never did. As he walked past his car, his mom opened an upstairs window and yelled, "You're walking to work, Avner?"

"Yeah."

"Your car isn't working, again?"

"It's fine. I want the exercise."

"You could have driven with your father."

"He goes in too early. And it's only a couple of kilometers."

Avner didn't want the exercise. He wanted the massive payout Geneviève's boss was going to give him for helping "relocate" artifacts. Leaving his car in the museum's parking lot after it closed would make him an immediate suspect when the heist was discovered. So he walked to work.

As Avner made his way to the museum, he thought about the details of the heist. He was nervous. *If I get caught, I'm going straight to prison for God knows how long. Ha! Did I just think about God? I don't even believe in God. Doesn't matter. I'm not getting caught! And after I pull this off, I'm going to buy a brand-new Ferrari. Geneviève should like that.*

When the museum closed that evening, Avner went into his office and locked the door. He walked into the closet to verify that everything he would need for the heist was still in its place. *Black sweatpants. Check. Hooded sweatshirt. Check. Ski mask. Check. Black plastic gloves. Check. Flashlight. Check. Microphone and earpiece to communicate with Ahmed and Gershom. Check. Loaded Glock 9mm. Check.*

He placed a large roll of bubble wrap, a utility knife, and a roll of black gaffing tape into the wood crate that Ahmed had shipped to him a few days earlier.

I'm good to go. I'll just turn off the lights, hang out in the closet, and wait for Ahmed to take out the power.

A half an hour later, Avner heard his office door slowly open.

What the heck? Who is that? Avner felt his heart begin to pound. Fearing the worst, he expected the police to open the closet door any second with guns drawn. But instead, he heard plastic rustling in his office.

What's going on? He leaned against the closet door to listen.

A man was humming. *I recognize that voice—it's Oren, the janitor. He must be collecting trash. Phew!*

Avner was relieved for a moment. But then Oren said, "Ah, there's a dolly. I was looking for one of these!"

Oh no, Avner thought, *I need that dolly!* He heard Oren wheel it out of his office and shut the door.

Dang it!

After the office door shut, Avner unmuted his wireless microphone. "Come in, Gershom. Are you there?"

Gershom Haddad was the museum's chief security officer. He had agreed to help Avner with the heist for $250,000 USD by misdirecting his overnight team of security guards.

"I'm here," Gershom said.

"It's Avner. Hey, Oren, the janitor just came in and—"

"Did he see you?"

"No, but he took the dolly! I can't collect the artifacts without it."

Gershom said, "All right, I'll try to find another one."

. . .

Later that evening, Eeman and Ahmed drove a large delivery truck down a dirt road five miles east of Jerusalem. When they arrived at the drone launch site deep inside a dark forest, they

Israel Museum, Jerusalem

quickly pulled the drone out and set it on the ground. Eeman held a flashlight while Ahmed opened a black metal box. Ahmed carefully pulled out a gray bomb and loaded it into the drone. After he loaded the fourth bomb, Ahmed climbed back into the truck's cab and began tapping keys on his laptop.

. . .

Back at the museum, Avner waited in his closet. Gershom had found another **dolly** and brought it to Avner's office. Ahmed's voice came in on Avner's earpiece.

"Checking in with you, Avner. This is Ahmed. Still there?"

"I'm here."

"Gershom, you there?"

"I'm here, Ahmed."

"It's 2:10 a.m. I'll be taking down power in five minutes," Ahmed said.

Avner quickly put on his ski mask and pulled the black sweats over his street clothes. He slid his loaded 9mm Glock 19 into a holster on his backside.

"Here we go, boys!" Ahmed said. "Power shutdown happening in 5, 4, 3, 2, 1. And now the backup auxiliary power, in 5, 4, 3, 2, 1. Too easy."

Eeman could be heard in the background. "You're good, Ahmed. Real good."

"We've gone black," Gershom said. "Great work, Ahmed."

Avner opened his closet door and could see that the tiny lights on his computer and

printer were off. He walked over to his office door and peeked out the small window. Total darkness. He could hear Gershom in his earpiece speaking to his eight-man security team on their walkie-talkies. "Men, this is Gershom. The power will probably be restored soon. I want each of you to head outside and stand by the exits of the buildings. Secure the perimeters of the buildings. Report to me when you're at a door."

A few minutes later, Gershom told Avner, "The building is yours. Time to roll."

"Thank you, my friend. Let's do this!" He propped his office door open, put the crate on the dolly, and wheeled it into the hallway. He quickly made his way toward the archaeological wing of the museum. As Avner closed in on the Jesus of Nazareth exhibit, he was glad to see that none of the red lights were blinking on the security cameras. He whispered to Ahmed, "You're a genius, Ahmed. You shut it all down."

"I do my best."

Avner arrived at the Jesus of Nazareth exhibit, laid the dolly down, and opened the crate. He quickly wrapped the artifacts in bubble wrap and placed them inside. He closed the lid and rolled the dolly away. "Three down," Avner whispered. "Two more to go."

"You're making great time," Ahmed said.

A few minutes later, Avner pulled the David Inscription out of its case, wrapped it in bubble wrap, and laid it in the crate.

"Gershom, you there? This is Avner."

"I am."

"I have the first four artifacts in the crate. Implement the next phase."

"Implementing the next phase now."

Ahmed came on. "Tremendous work, Avner. The drone is up and on its way to the museum."

Avner heard Gershom talking to his men on his walkie-talkie. "Men, change in thinking. I want everyone to come back inside. There are only eight of you. I want you to focus on the art wing. In the unlikely chance that thieves are behind this power outage, they'll surely go after the paintings. Several of them are worth millions of dollars. So again, report to the art wing immediately."

A couple of minutes later, Gershom told Avner, "You're clear. My men are with the paintings. Go!"

Avner rolled the crate outside and headed toward the Shrine of the Book, where the Dead Sea Scrolls are stored. He whispered to Gershom, "No guards. Thank you."

Ahmed came on. "Drone will be arriving in three minutes."

Avner unlocked a side door into the Shrine, parked the crate inside, and hurried downstairs to the vault. He looked at the entry code on a piece of paper, punched it in, and turned

the handle.

"Boom! I'm in the vault, guys."

Avner pulled the **Isaiah Scroll** off a long shelf and said, "I'm rolling up the Isaiah Scroll."

"You're doing great," Ahmed said. "Right on schedule. Drone ETA is 60 seconds. I'll hit the data center and then pick up the crate. Let me know when it's in position."

Avner said, "I'm sliding the scroll into the tube." But he noticed something in the upper corner of the vault. He quickly turned away, walked out, and shut the heavy metal door. As he ran up the stairs, he said, "Ahmed! Why was there a red light blinking on the camera in the vault? I thought you killed the auxiliary power."

"Serious? It must be running on an internal battery."

"Dang it!"

"Calm down. You have a mask on, right?"

"Right, but I talked and my voice—"

"I'm going to take out the data center. Get moving!"

Avner laid the tube in the crate, closed the latches, and wheeled it outside. "I'm outside. I'm bringing the crate to the pick-up location."

"Copy. Drone ETA is 30 seconds," Ahmed responded.

"Heads up, guys!" Gershom said, panicked. "One of the security guards said he heard something and went outside to check on it."

"Tell him to get back inside!" Ahmed yelled.

"I did! He's not responding!"

"Ahmed," Avner said, "after you take out the data center, the crate is in position and ready for pick up."

"The guard will have a clear line of sight to the pick-up location in about 20 seconds," Gershom said.

"We don't have time to take out the data center," Ahmed yelled. "We'll have to come back later!"

"What?" Avner whispered angrily.

"We need to get the artifacts out of there before the guard comes around that corner and interferes with the relocation," Ahmed said. "I'm lowering the cable. Attach the hook to the crate. I'll bring the artifacts back to the truck, then fly the drone back. Hurry!"

"Whatever!" Avner said. "Lower the cable a tad. A little more . . . that's good." He slid the iron hook through the ring that had cables fastened to all four corners of the crate. "All right, the hook is through the ring. Take it away!"

Avner ran and crouched behind a nearby bush. He heard the drone's propellers overhead and watched the crate lift off the ground. He repositioned himself in the bushes to keep an eye out for the guard and pulled his gun out of its holster. Avner whispered into his mic, "I see the guard, Gershom! See if you can say something to get him back inside. I need to get out of here."

The guard walked around with his flashlight for a couple

of minutes, looking at the buildings. Then he ran back toward the art wing. *Did Gershom say something? Did the guard see something? I don't have time to find out.*

As soon as the guard disappeared around the corner, Avner took off like a gazelle. He angled across the museum property and down a hill with trees on the museum's east side. He stopped halfway down the hill, pulled off his black sweats, mask, and gloves, and dropped them in a hole he dug a few days earlier. He filled it with the original dirt, caught his breath, and looked up. He was glad to see that the drone was gone.

Ahmed's voice came in over his earpiece. "Avner, are you there?"

"I'm here."

"Good work! The drone is on its way back to us. As we discussed previously, cut across Rehavia Park, and make your way to the Jerusalem Medical Center. Your ride will arrive in a couple of minutes."

"Thank you, but please tell me again that you'll be flying the drone back tonight to take out the data center."

"Absolutely, my friend. This is only a tiny hiccup in the plan!"

"If you don't, Ahmed, they're going to have video footage of me in the vault. And if I go to prison over this, I'll opt for a lighter sentence by telling them everything I know about you guys."

"Rest easy, dude! We'll be back to take out the data center."

"Thank you."

"I have to go," Ahmed said. "The drone and the crate are coming in right now. I'll be in touch soon."

• • •

Ahmed guided the drone toward the truck and slowly lowered the crate to the ground. Eeman unhooked it from the drone. Ahmed retracted the cable with a tap on his iPad and brought the drone to the ground. But he noticed something he had not anticipated. The drone's battery level was down to 32 percent. He muted his mic and looked at Eeman. "Bummer! Carrying all that weight really drained the battery. There's no way it can make another round trip to the museum without a recharge. We'll have to take it back to the house and charge it for two or three hours."

"I'd say that's more than a hiccup in the plan. That's more like a long burp, like this . . ."

Ahmed stared at him and shook his head. "You're gross!"

Eeman grinned. "So we'll recharge the drone and drive back here for another flight?"

"We'll have to."

"You know there's going to be police at the museum by then."

"Yeah, probably. But if we don't take out the data center, Avner's going down. And he'll take us with him."

They folded the drones' arms, lifted it, and slid it into the truck.

"Shouldn't we take the bombs out?" Eeman asked.

"They'll be fine."

"On the bumpy dirt road out of here?"

"Yeah, they'll be okay."

"I hope those aren't Ahmed's famous last words."

"They won't be. Because if the bombs blow, no one will

know I said them. Right? So relax," Ahmed said with a smile.

"Yeah, relax. Your words are very comforting," Eeman said.

They picked up the wood crate and loaded it next to the drone. Ahmed pulled down the truck's door and locked it. "Let's go!"

• • •

When they arrived at the house in Herzliya, Eeman backed the truck up to the garage door. He and Ahmed slid the crate out and brought it into the living room.

"Make some coffee, Eeman. I'll plug the drone in. Then we'll open the crate."

Ahmed's phone rang. It was Radomir.

"Good morning, Boss."

"It's not morning here in England. But how'd it go? Did Avner get the artifacts?"

"I believe so. Eeman and I are back at the house with the crate. I was just about to open it."

"Please do. And switch me over to FaceTime so that I can see them."

"All right. Switching to FaceTime. Can you see?"

"I can."

"Eeman, hold my phone."

Ahmed unhooked the latches on all four sides of the lid, removed the top, and peeled away some of the bubble wrap.

"Oh my," Ahmed said, "this is the inscription that mentions David." He picked it up, admired the small Aramaic letters inscribed on it, and rotated it for Radomir to see it.

"Wow. It's beautiful!" Radomir said. "I have great plans for you, David!"

Out of view of the camera, Eeman rolled his eyes and silently mouthed to Ahmed, "He's so weird!"

Ahmed reached into the crate and pulled out a white cylinder. "Inside this tube should be the Isaiah Scroll."

"Don't pull the scroll out," Radomir warned. "It's too fragile. Just pull the plastic cap off and let me look inside."

Ahmed pulled the cap off, and Eeman moved the phone so Radomir could see the top edges of the ancient scroll.

"I'm getting goosebumps," Radomir said. "I can't wait to touch you, ancient scroll of Isaiah. You're going to look so good on my wall!" He was equally as excited over the Pontius Pilate inscription, Caiaphas's ossuary, and the heel bone with a spike in it.

When Radomir finished looking at the artifacts, Ahmed explained the need to fly the drone back to take out the data center.

"Well, that's regrettable," Radomir said. "I trust you will not disappoint me on the next attempt."

• • •

Ahmed checked on the drone's battery an hour later. It was at 80 percent. Fighting off a yawn, he looked at Eeman who was asleep on the couch. "Hey! Wake up. The battery's good. Let's go!"

Halfway back to the remote launch site they'd used earlier, Eeman looked in his mirror and said, "You've got to be kidding me. A cop is pulling us over!"

"Seriously?" Ahmed asked. "How fast were you driving?"

"I don't know, like 115 in a 100 zone."

"Dang it, Eeman! All right, play it cool. Thankfully, the artifacts are back at the house. What are we doing? Uh, it's a Wednesday morning, and we're on our way to help a friend move."

The police officer came up to the passenger side window and asked for Eeman's ID and other paperwork. "Do you know how fast you were driving?"

"Too fast?" Eeman asked.

"Too fast. Where you men headed?"

Eeman was so nervous he forgot what Ahmed told him to say. "We're going to the museum in Jerusalem."

Ahmed nearly had a heart attack.

"The Israel Museum? This early? It doesn't open until 10 a.m.," the officer said.

"A different museum that opens earlier," Eeman clarified.

Ahmed coughed and said, "Actually, officer, we're helping a friend move this morning. And then we're going to a museum later today."

"Well," the officer said, "there was a robbery at the Israel Museum earlier this morning. It might not be open today. You should call them first."

Eeman said, "Yes, we should call them. I hope they catch the men who stole the artifacts." Realizing how dumb that was, he looked ashamedly at Ahmed and said, "Or the *women* who stole the artifacts."

"Or the paintings, or whatever items they might have stolen," Ahmed added, trying to fix the statement.

"All right, guys, slow it down," the officer said. "Be safe, and good luck with the move."

"Yes, the move," Eeman said. "We're happy to help relocate people's stuff."

As the officer walked back to his car, Ahmed shook his head. "You big oaf. Let me do the talking next time!"

They arrived at the secluded launch site a short while later and pulled out the drone. Ahmed looked at his watch. It was 9:08 a.m. As they expanded the drone's arms, they heard the voices of women talking.

Eeman looked at Ahmed. "What in the world? There are people out here?"

Ahmed said, "Get the drone back in the truck!"

It was too late. Four women hikers walked by. A couple of the ladies said, "Good morning!"

Paralyzed by the surprise, Ahmed said, "Um . . . hello, ladies."

"Don't mind us," Eeman said. "We're not doing anything illegal."

The ladies smiled and kept walking. But a few seconds later, a lady turned around and said, "That drone is huge! What brand is it? My son loves drones. I'll tell him about it."

"Please don't!" Ahmed snapped.

Eeman lowered his voice and said, "Ma'am, we're with the Iraqi Armed Forc…"

"IDF!" Ahmed interrupted. "We're with the Israel Defense Force."

Eeman nodded. "Yeah, that one. I used to be in the Iraqi one."

"He's kidding!" Ahmed said. "We're with IDF, and we're conducting a test. I need to ask you to keep this encounter to yourself for national security's sake."

"Oh, I will," the lady said. "My friends and I so appreciate the IDF. Thank you for your service!"

"You're welcome."

Ahmed tapped a button on his iPad, and all six of the drone's propellers whirled and kicked up dirt and pine needles. The woman hurried off. The drone took off and flew east toward the museum. Its cameras transmitted live video back to Ahmed's iPad. When it reached the museum, Ahmed told Eeman, "There are about a dozen police cars at the museum and what appears to be a press conference out front." He adjusted its positioning over the data center and said, "Sorry to interrupt your morning news program . . . dropping bombs in 5, 4 . . . "

Eeman looked over Ahmed's shoulder. "Wait! Do you think anyone's in there?"

"I don't know. But if we don't light up this building, you, me, and Avner are going to jail."

"Do it!"

"Releasing bombs one, two, three, and four."

A few seconds later, the two-story white-stone and glass building exploded.

Eeman's phone rang. It was Radomir. "Hey, Boss."

"Put me on speaker so Ahmed can hear. . . . I'm watching the drone's transmission on my computer. That was a direct hit, Ahmed! Beautiful."

"Thanks, Boss. I'm pulling out—the police are shooting at the drone."

"Wait. What's that helicopter there?" Radomir asked.

"It's a police helicopter."

"They might try to get that thing in the air and follow the drone straight back to you guys."

"That's a possibility, Boss."

"Take it out!"

"At your bidding."

Ahmed rotated the drone with a couple of taps and unleashed a torrent of bullets on the helicopter. The bullets shattered its windshield, engine, and rotor blades.

Radomir yelled, "Yes! Yes!"

As fire and smoke billowed out of the aircraft, Ahmed directed the drone to soar straight up about 1,000 feet and then west, back toward the truck. As soon as the drone landed, Ahmed and Eeman loaded it into the truck and sped off down the dirt road. As they neared the bottom of the hill, they saw the women hikers on the side of the road. Eeman slowed down the truck and rolled down his window.

"It was nice to meet you ladies. We had a blast!" He rolled up his window and continued driving.

"You *want* us to go to jail, don't you?" Ahmed said.

"Of course not. Why would you think that?"

Ahmed shook his head. "Take me back to the house."

Chapter 15

Dakota was in the backyard cleaning the pool when he heard his mom yell, "Kids, you've got to come watch the news!"

"What's going on?" Dakota yelled.

"The museum we were at a couple of days ago was robbed last night and then bombed this morning!"

"Whaaat?"

The Knoxes gathered around Abigail's computer on the kitchen table. They watched a news reporter at the museum explain what artifacts were missing and what the drone had done during the press conference.

Dakota pointed at the screen. "Look at the fire and smoke coming out of that building behind her!"

"Wow, kids, just wow!" Abigail said. "That's where we just were."

"We saw those artifacts during our tour!" Hank said.

Dakota could hardly believe what he was seeing. "Mom, remember Sunday? Afton and I went to the security office, and I told them about that suspicious employee."

"I remember. You think that's the thief?"

"I don't know, but I bet he knew about this. They're going to catch him! I have to text Afton."

> **Dakota:** Hey Afton, good morning. Crazy stuff is happening in the news. Are you able to come over?

> **Afton:** I'll come over!

Dakota: Did you save the museum security chief's business card?

Afton: Yes!

Dakota: Can you bring it with you? The door is unlocked. We're in the living room.

Dakota turned on the television and sat down on the couch to watch the news. His mom, siblings, and Afton soon joined him.

After watching a couple of minutes of the coverage, Afton turned to Dakota and said, "Oh, my gosh, Dakota! Do you think the guy we reported to security was behind this?"

"I don't know. But I'm glad we talked to the chief of security. You brought his card?"

"Yes, here it is. Gershom Haddad."

"I'm going to call him and remind him of our meeting."

"You should call the police tip line, too."

"For sure."

Dakota left detailed voicemails for Gershom and the police. His mom said, "I'm sure they'll be calling you back soon."

Chapter 16
Monday, June 13, Herzliya.

Five days later, Dakota and Afton were walking along the **beach boardwalk** back to their neighborhood.

"Ice cream in a waffle cone is the best," Dakota said.

"I agree. Waffle cones are way better than cups and spoons but terribly messy!"

"Yeah! You have ice cream on your nose."

"I do?" Afton asked.

"Yes!"

"Well, you have it on your chin."

Dakota felt his chin. "No, I don't."

"You do now!" Afton said as she tapped the top of her ice cream against his chin.

"Hey, now!"

She took off running, laughing. Dakota chased her as well as he could in flip-flops. When he caught up to her, she surrendered. "I'm sorry! I couldn't resist."

"I hope you like Rocky Road!" He moved his cone toward her face.

"The Bible says not to repay evil for evil!" Afton said.

Dakota laughed and lowered his cone. "All right, I won't get you back. Not because of that verse. But because I don't want to waste a single bite of this deliciousness."

They sat down on a bench and wiped themselves off with napkins.

Afton said, "Hey, did the police department or the security chief respond to your messages yet?"

"No, and it's super frustrating. The police department asks for tips, but then they don't follow up with them. What's up with that? I think I know who stole the artifacts, or at least the guy who might know who did it. And apparently, they don't care."

"What are you going to do?"

"I'm going to start my own investigation."

"Really? How?"

"Well, I'm going to find out all I can about that Avner guy. Maybe he accidentally left some clues that he was involved with the heist."

"How are you going to do that?"

"Well, I bet he's on Facebook or some other form of social media. So, I was thinking I'd start there by seeing what I could discover about him. Maybe I'll do that later tonight. I need to install Facebook on my phone."

"I have Facebook on my phone," Afton said. "I never use it, but I have it. Why don't I do a search for him right now? His name was Avner, right?

"Right. It's not a very common name."

"Okay, hold my ice cream," Afton said.

For the next couple of minutes, they looked at the profile pictures on Afton's phone.

"There he is!" Dakota said. "I recognize his face."

"His current city is Jerusalem," Afton said. "But what next?"

"We study his posts, find out where he's been, what he likes, where he hangs out. But not now. Your ice cream is melting. We can do that back at the house."

They walked back to the Knoxes' house, rinsed their sticky hands, and sat down at a table in the backyard by the pool.

Afton said, "Why don't you scroll through Avner's posts on my phone, and I'll take notes?"

"That sounds good."

For the next 30 minutes, Dakota looked at every one of Avner's photos and captions. They tried his Instagram account next, but it was private.

"Well, we can't access his Instagram posts," Dakota said, "but his Facebook posts are pretty insightful."

"Here's what we know about him," Afton said. "He works at the Israel Museum in Jerusalem. His dad is the director of the museum. He likes to get coffee at a place called Aroma. He drives a 2014 white Toyota Corolla with tinted windows and black rims. He's an atheist. He thinks Christians are idiots. He owns a black Glock handgun. He likes to go to the gym. He posts lots of selfies. And it appears that he's single. *That's* not surprising."

"Why do you say that?" Dakota asked.

"Girls can tell he's a creep. He posts loads of selfies, pictures of himself flexing at the gym, partying, holding a gun. No girl is going to settle down and start a family with this guy."

"Not your type, huh?"

"Not my type."

Dakota looked at Afton. "You think you'll ever get married and start a family?"

"I'd like to get married someday, but I'll wait for the right person."

"Yeah, same."

Hank walked into the backyard. "Hey guys, Ethan's coming over, and we're going to swim in the pool."

"Okay," Dakota said. "Where's everyone else?"

"Mom and Dad went out for dinner, and Jalynn is spending the night with that weird family next door."

Afton looked up.

"Oh, I'm sorry, Afton!" Hank said, laughing.

"Hilarious, Hank," Afton said.

"What are you two up to?" Hank asked.

"We're trying to figure out if the guy at the museum is behind the theft of the artifacts," Dakota said.

"Oh! That sounds more fun than swimming. Can Ethan and I help?"

"Maybe. I think we could use your help in a day or two if we find some good leads."

"Sounds good," Hank said as he skimmed the surface of the pool with a net.

Dakota told Afton, "Maybe we visit the museum and try to talk to him, ask him some questions."

"He won't be there. They've temporarily closed the museum. Remember?"

"I forgot that. Let's see if he's on any other social media apps. How about TikTok?"

After a couple of minutes of searching, Afton found Avner's TikTok account, and they started watching his videos.

"He's certainly strange," Afton said.

"Look at that. Pause it," Dakota said as he pointed at the video on her phone. "There's a street sign there in the background as he's walking around his neighborhood. I'll look that up on my phone. . . . He lives about 2 miles southeast of the museum in Jerusalem. You up for a drive tonight?"

"I'm up for it."

Hank overheard and said, "So are we! Right, Ethan?"

Ethan, who had just walked into the backyard, responded, "Sure!"

"We'll sit in the back," Hank said, "and you'll hardly know we're there."

"What are we doing?" Ethan asked.

"I'd like to scout out the house of the employee that I reported to museum security," Dakota told him. "If his car is out front, maybe I'll take a photo of the license plate—you know, a little reconnaissance mission."

"Recona . . . what?" Ethan asked.

Dakota clarified. "It's a simple observation and research mission."

"What good will that do in catching a thief?" Ethan asked.

"I don't know for sure," Dakota said. "But watching you guys swim isn't going to help us track down a thief. So I'm thinking we go scout out where this guy lives and see if it leads to anything."

"Exactly, Dakota!" Hank said. "And maybe we stop for dinner somewhere."

"All right, I'm up for it," Ethan said.

A couple of minutes later, the four of them were seated in the red Bronco. Dakota started the engine.

"Oops. Sorry, I forgot something," Hank said. "I need to go get it." He ran back inside and returned a minute later.

"All right," Hank said, "let's go."

On the way to Jerusalem, Afton said, "It's a beautiful night for a drive to Jerusalem. I've never seen the old city at night." She looked up through the front windshield and said, "The stars look amazing tonight. It's so clear out. You can really see them."

"I love looking at the stars," Dakota replied. "I read a quote recently by Abraham Lincoln. I forget the exact wording, but basically, he said, 'I can see how it might be possible for a person to look down upon the earth and be an atheist, but I cannot see how a person could look up into the heavens and say there is no God.'"

"That's good," Afton said. "I agree. How could all those stars and planets come from nothing and by nothing? That seems absurd. There must be a creator. Speaking of God. I've been reading the Gospel of Luke the last few days."

"That's cool."

"Yeah, I'm loving it. Jesus is amazing! But I told a friend back home that I was reading it, and she said, 'The Gospels were written 300 years after Jesus lived.' I didn't know what to say."

"When someone makes a claim like that," Dakota said, "I like to start my response by asking, 'How did you come to that conclusion?' or 'What evidence is there for that?' Often, they can't support their claims with any good evidence or reasons why I should take their position seriously. And they seem to be slightly more open to what I have to say regarding the matter."

"That's good. I didn't think of doing that."

"Regarding your friend's claim about the Gospels being written three centuries after Jesus lived, it's totally false. The church fathers, leaders in the early Christian church, were already quoting the New Testament in their writings in the second century. So we know the New Testament was done by then. But there's good evidence most of the New Testament was written down before AD 70."

"Really?"

"Yeah. For example, the New Testament Scriptures are silent regarding the Romans' destruction of the Jewish temple in AD 70."

"Why is that significant?" Afton asked.

"Well, the destruction of the temple in Jerusalem was one of the most significant events in Jewish history. Flavius Josephus, an eyewitness to the event, said the Roman soldiers destroyed the Jewish temple and the entire city of Jerusalem. It was crazy! Josephus said 1.1 million people died and that the Romans carried away 97,000 people as prisoners."

"Wow!"

"Well, the silence of the New Testament authors regarding that event strongly suggests their writings were largely completed prior to this event."

"I get that. Because they would have mentioned it if they wrote after it took place."

"Yes! And we know from historical sources that Paul was put to death around AD 64 and Peter around AD 65. And though the deaths of other prominent Christians are mentioned in the New Testament, the deaths of Peter and Paul are not mentioned anywhere. That seems to indicate the New Testament was mostly completed before these two leaders in the church were put to death. So, those are a couple of reasons why scholars have concluded the Gospels were completed while the eyewitnesses of Jesus's life were still alive."

"That's interesting, Dakota, and helpful. Thank you."

A short while later, they arrived in the neighborhood where they thought Avner might live. It was an upscale area with lots of large, renovated homes.

Dakota drove the Bronco slowly down the street. "Look for a white Toyota Corolla."

They drove the length of the street three times. No Corolla.

"All right," Dakota said. "Sorry, you guys. Maybe they've moved, or he drives a different car now."

"It's okay," Afton said. "We tried."

"Let's go get something to eat," Hank said.

Dakota stopped at a stop sign and put his blinker on to turn left.

"Wait!" Afton said. "That's a white car coming toward us."

Hank said, "And it has black rims."

"That's the car!" Dakota said. "All right, remain calm. We'll go park over here and let him park. We don't want him to see us following him."

A couple of minutes later, Dakota drove down the street again. The Corolla was parked in the driveway of a charming two-story stone house.

"All right, let's park here, about 100 yards away," Dakota said. "And then we'll walk past the house and get a closer look." Dakota turned the engine off. "All right, look casual. Let's go."

They got out of the car and tried their best to look calm as they walked down the neighborhood street. When they got near the vehicle, Dakota began to video Hank and Ethan in such a way that the car and the front of the house ended up in the video. A minute later, they turned around and headed back toward the Bronco. When they walked past the Corolla, Hank turned and walked about fifteen feet up the driveway. He reached out his hand and looked like he was trying to open the Corolla's trunk.

Dakota couldn't believe it. He whispered loudly, "Hank! What are you doing? Stop!" Hank hurried back to the sidewalk. As they got closer to the Bronco, Dakota said, "Bro, what were you thinking? You shouldn't have touched the car. You could have set off an alarm or left fingerprints."

Hank said, "I'm sorry, Dak. Please forgive me. I was just—"

"If you want to help us with the investigation, you're going to need to listen carefully for *what* to do and what *not* to do. Anyhow, love you, bro. I forgive you. Let's go get some food. I hope they didn't have a security camera out front."

Chapter 17
Tuesday, June 14, Herzliya.

The next morning, Dakota was cutting up fruit in the kitchen. Hank was working on his laptop on the counter.

"It looks like Avner is at a place called Aroma," Hank said.

Dakota froze. He looked at Hank and said, "Wait, what?"

Hank looked at Dakota with a big grin.

"How do you know that? Is he live on Facebook?" Dakota asked.

"Facebook? I'm 14. No one my age uses Facebook. I'm tracking him."

"Tracking him?"

"Yeah, as we were about to drive to Jerusalem last night, I had the idea to run inside and take off one of the tiny tracking devices Dad put on our suitcases. I put a piece of tape on it, and I stuck it on Avner's car."

"You . . . attached . . . a . . . GPS . . . luggage tracker . . . to Avner's car?" He lowered his voice and whispered, "That's totally illegal, Hank!"

"It is?"

"In the U.S., it is. I don't know about Israel. But I bet it is!"

"Ooh, I didn't know."

"Well, you're brilliant to have thought of that, but we have to obey the law."

"Yeah, for sure. I didn't know it might be illegal."

"Well, don't do that again, please."

Dakota went back to cutting fruit. Then he set the knife down and walked over to Hank. "Where'd you say Avner is?"

"Well, he was just at a place called Aroma, buying cologne or something."

Dakota laughed. "Cologne! Aroma is a café where people buy *coffee*—not cologne! You crack me up."

Hank said, "Well, he must have got his coffee already because he's leaving."

"Where's he going?" Dakota asked.

"He's on the highway headed toward Herzliya."

"Seriously?"

"Yep," Hank said. "Maybe he tracked *us!* Maybe he saw us on a security camera, and he's headed here with a gun to kill us."

133

"No, stop! He's not going to do that," Dakota insisted. Then he remembered the pictures he and Afton had seen of Avner holding a gun. "On second thought," Dakota said, "I'll go make sure the gate to the driveway is shut. Keep an eye on that tracker!"

Chapter 18

After Radomir verified that the artifacts were safely in Ahmed and Eeman's possession, he made good on his promise to pay Avner. Radomir thought $2,500,000 was an excellent deal for the five artifacts. He had been ready to pay more if Avner had negotiated a higher price, but he hadn't.

When the money showed up in Avner's bitcoin account, he could hardly believe it. He was elated for about 24 hours. The joy fizzled when he realized how difficult it would be to spend the money without raising suspicions. He was also under investigation by the Israel Police Department, as was every museum employee. He thought being the museum director's son, acting brokenhearted over the loss of the artifacts, and zealously offering to help with the investigation would rule him out as a suspect. It didn't.

So Avner was depressed and afraid. He laid in bed every night after the heist, fearing that police officers were going to kick open his door and arrest him. Not having any friends he could confide in, he explained his predicament, by text message, to one of the few people who would understand— Ahmed. Two days passed without a response.

Tuesday, June 14,
Aroma Espresso Bar, Jerusalem.

Avner sat by himself in a café sulking over a cappuccino and picking at a chocolate croissant. A message popped up on his phone. It was from Ahmed. *Finally!*

> **Ahmed:** Sorry for the delay, Avner. Where are you? Can you talk?

> **Avner:** Texting would be better. I'm at Aroma café in Jerusalem.

> **Ahmed:** I talked to Robert about your dilemma, and he'd like to make you an offer I think you're going to love! He wants to hire you, give you a new life and identity in England. Why don't you drive down here to Herzliya? I'll tell you more in person.

> **Avner:** Wow! Sounds interesting. I'd love to talk. I'll come right now.

He got up from his chair at Aroma and drove off toward Herzliya.

• • •

As Hank continued to track Avner, Dakota messaged Afton:

Hey Afton! Good morning. Who's home at your place?

Afton: Just me and Ethan. My dad is at work. My mom is running errands with Evelyn.

Dakota: Can you and Ethan come over ASAP? Long story, but we've tracked Avner, and it looks like he's coming to Herzliya and will be here in about ten minutes! Don't panic, but please come over.

Afton: On our way. Cutting through the backyard.

Dakota: Okay. Come up to the game room.

When the Hansleys arrived, Dakota shut and locked the door.

"Does anyone have a gun?" Ethan asked.

"No. Let's stay calm," Dakota said. "I have a hard time believing Avner's coming after us. But it *is* odd that he's driving in this direction the night after we scouted out his house. So, to be safe, I thought it would be best for us to all be together."

He explained how Hank had attached a GPS tracker to Avner's car.

Ethan gave Hank a high five. "That's amazing, Hank!"

"Well, Dak said it's illegal. So I won't be doing it again."

"But it might save our lives," Ethan said.

Hank gave another update. "Avner's getting closer, probably arriving in Hertz . . . Can we just call this town *Hertz*? I'm tired of pronouncing it *Hertzselleeuh*!"

"Agreed!" Ethan said. "Thank you, Hank. One-syllable city

names are way easier!"

"That's fine with me," Dakota said. "What's his ETA Hank?"

"Two minutes."

"You know what?" Dakota said. "Why don't we put the couch in front of the game room door just to be safe?"

They all jumped up and helped move it.

"And from this window over here," Dakota said, "we can look out over the neighborhood and watch for his car."

Dakota, Afton, and Ethan walked over to the window and peeked out the blinds.

Hank stared wide-eyed at his computer. "Uh, guys, Avner's definitely coming into our neighborhood."

Dakota felt his heart rate speed up.

"Oh boy, you guys, he's coming down our street!" Hank said.

Dakota pulled out his phone. "I should call the police."

"Oh, my goodness," Afton said. She bowed her head. "God, we pray that You will keep us safe. We don't know what we're doing. We don't have any guns. We look to *You* for protection and wisdom. In Jesus's name, we pray. Amen!"

Dakota's heart slowed down. He looked at Afton, smiled, and said, "Amen! Thank you."

The white Corolla stopped about 75 yards from the Knoxes' house. They all looked at each other.

"Maybe God gave him a flat tire," Hank said.

"No. Look," Dakota said, "he's turning into that house's driveway."

Hank got up and joined them at the window.

Afton said, "He must have a friend or relative who lives there."

"Or partners in crime," Dakota said.

They monitored the house from the window for about a half-hour. Then Dakota said, "Well, we know Avner didn't come here to kill us. I think I'll put on some sunglasses and a hat and go for a little bike ride."

"I'm coming," Afton said.

They walked downstairs. Dakota grabbed his sunglasses, a couple of baseball caps, and a pair of Jalynn's sunglasses. "You can wear these, Afton. Jalynn would be honored for you to wear her Padres hat."

"Padres? Is that what the SD stands for?"

"Yeah, San Diego Padres. It's our hometown baseball team."

"Oh, I thought it might stand for something different."

"Like South Dakota or something?"

"Hmm, close. Maybe I'll tell you someday. Let's roll."

They pedaled the bikes down the street. The driveway gate at the house where Avner parked was open. Dakota and Afton could see the Corolla parked next to a white transport truck and a black Range Rover.

"That's definitely the car we saw last night," Afton said. "What do you think we should do?"

"I just had an idea. Let's head back."

They parked the bikes in the garage and went back to the game room.

"All right, guys, I have an idea," Dakota said. "Let me know what you think. Tomorrow, I go to the house and ask whoever lives there if they'd like any yard work done. I'll bring a rake and a weed eater and totally look the part."

Ethan rolled his eyes. "What will that accomplish?"

"If they answer the door, that will allow me to see who lives there. That might not lead to anything, but you never know. What do you guys think?"

"I like it," Hank said. Afton agreed.

• • •

While the Knox and Hansley kids discussed their plans, Ahmed explained Radomir's offer to Avner inside the house down the street.

"Yes, you're going to have a hard time spending all that money here in Israel. The authorities would be very suspicious. Radom . . . excuse me, Robert is sympathetic to your situation, Avner. He likes you. You got the artifacts for him, and he was very impressed. He'd like to hire you to work for him in England as part of his inner circle."

"With you and Eeman?"

"Yes, and a few others. He'll pay you a nice salary. We'll set you up with a new identity. You can live in his mansion—you can have a new start. It's like what Eeman and I agreed to. But it requires that you move to England. Would you be interested in that?"

"Wow! Yes. I'm honored. What's the salary? I mean, I don't *need* the money with two and a half million dollars in the bank, but I'm curious," Avner said.

"You're not a good negotiator, are you?" Ahmed said.

"Horrible."

Ahmed laughed. "Yeah, well, the pay would be 100,000 pounds a year, about 450,000 shekels."

"That's generous. I'll do it!"

"Well, here's the thing, Avner. Israeli authorities are finally

139

lifting the marina and airport lockdown that they implemented after the heist. They're allowing people to leave the country, starting tomorrow. So Eeman and I are sailing to England tomorrow. You can join us in England later if you can get there. But you're under investigation and might be arrested if you wait. I hope not. But I'd advise you to sneak out of Israel with us tomorrow. We have secret compartments on the yacht where you can hide. Once you're in the U.K., you can start your new life, be free to spend your money, and so on. What do you think?"

"I'll do it. I'll sail with you and Eeman tomorrow."

"Very good."

"I'll drive home, grab a few things, give my parents a hug."

"Don't tell them you're leaving," Ahmed warned, "or where you're going."

"Of course."

"Eeman told his parents what country he was moving to, and let's just say Robert wasn't happy about it."

"Understood. What time do you want me here?"

"Eeman and I are going to refuel the boat tomorrow, prep it for the trip to England, load the artifacts, and—"

"Not in the crate."

"No, for sure not in the crate. We don't want to draw attention to ourselves on the dock. We're going to load them in duffel bags. We're planning to sail at 2:00 p.m. So try to be at the marina no later than 1:30 p.m. You'll see our yacht—it's the biggest one. Its name is *Poseidon's Dream*.

"I'll be there tomorrow!" Avner said. "Thank you, Ahmed."

The next day, Dakota, Afton, and Hank were in the Knoxes' game room or "Command Central," as Hank wanted to call it.

Ethan Hansley walked in and said, "Hey guys! I saw on the news that Israel and the museum are offering reward money— like a lot—for tips that lead to the recovery of the artifacts. Maybe we're going to get rich if this works out!"

"That's nice of them, Ethan, but we're not doing this for a reward," Dakota said.

Hank looked up from his computer. "Update on Avner. It appears that the GPS tracker fell off. Either that or his car has been parked on the side of the highway for hours."

"Okay, thanks, Hank," Dakota said. "I'm going to head over to the house and offer to do some yard work. Can we pray first? Hank, would you mind starting us?"

"Sure. Dear God, we ask that You'll keep Dakota from throwing out his back as he's pulling weeds. Just kidding. God, whatever happens over there when Dakota knocks on the door, keep him safe. We don't know who lives there, probably nobody dangerous. But You know. Give Dakota wisdom; we pray."

Afton prayed, "Heavenly Father, You love Dakota so much. Will You keep him safe? Surround him with Your mighty angels. And we pray for Your help with what we're trying to do. You know we don't care about the money or any kind of reward. We just want to help get those stolen artifacts back to the museum so they might be a blessing to people. Guide us, we pray, in Jesus's name. Amen."

"Amen! Thanks, guys." Dakota looked at his watch and said, "If I'm not back within an hour, call the police. It's 12:15 right now. Okay? At 1:15, call the police."

"We will, but you're going to be fine," Afton said.

Dakota gave her a fist bump. "Thank you."

"Be careful."

"I will."

He went to the garage and grabbed weed and hedge trimmers. As he walked toward the neighbor's house, he whispered some of the words from Psalm 23. "Even though I walk through the valley of the shadow of death, I will fear no evil; for You are with me. . . . Surely goodness and mercy shall follow me all the days of my life; and I will dwell in the house of the Lord forever."

Afton, Hank, and Ethan watched him from the game room window.

Dakota turned up the driveway and slowly walked toward the porch. It was a modern white house overlooking the ocean. He noticed that the Corolla and black Range Rover were gone. *Maybe they aren't home. Or perhaps someone is going to open the door and start shooting.*

He shook his head to clear his thoughts and said, "All right, God, here we go."

He walked up the steps and rang the doorbell. No response. He tried again.

A man inside yelled, "Come in!"

Really? Should I? He must be expecting someone else. Well, I'll at least open the door. Dakota cautiously opened the door and peeked in. There was no one there, so he took a few steps inside and said, "Hello."

From the bathroom near the kitchen, a man yelled, "Now you come? When I'm in the shower? I thought you forgot about me."

Dakota didn't know what to think or say, so he said, "Uh . . . sorry."

In a calmer voice, the man said, "You can leave the pizza on the dining table. The money is there. And keep the change. You don't deserve a tip but take it."

Dakota heard the shower water turn on and realized there was a huge mix-up happening. As he turned around to walk out, he noticed a large wood crate sitting on the carpet in the living room. *I wonder if there's a name on the shipping label. That might be a good lead.* He walked over to it, bent over, and looked at the label. Most of it had been torn off, but Dakota could still see the word *Museum* and part of the street address. *This crate was shipped to the Israel Museum in Jerusalem—what in the world?*

Dakota looked over at the bathroom door. It was closed, and the shower water was running. He laid the weed and hedge trimmers next to the crate. *What's in this thing?* He slid the wood lid off. Inside were heaps of bubble wrap. He quickly rummaged through it and felt something sturdy and heavy. He picked it up and began peeling away the plastic. As he did, he heard the shower water turn off. *Oh no! I only have a few more seconds.* He pulled off the last bit of wrap, and there in his hands was the 3,000-year-old David Inscription. *Good God!* He stared in disbelief, swallowed, and tears began to well up in his eyes. *I have to go, and this is coming with me!*

Dakota left the gardening tools in the living room and bolted out the door. With a leap that would have made his lacrosse coach proud, he cleared all six porch steps and sprinted up the street toward his house. Afton, Hank, and Ethan were glued to the upstairs window, wondering what was happening. He saw them as he ran up the driveway and yelled, "Shut the gate! Shut the gate!" He ran through the front door, yelling, "Woohoo! You guys! Mom! You're not going to believe it."

He turned around and locked the front door.

Afton and all the kids hurried down the stairs.

"What's happening?" Abigail asked.

"I found it! I found it!" He held up the stone slab for them to see. "I found the **David Inscription**!"

"What?"

"No way!"

"Woohoo! That's amazing!"

"Are you kidding me?"

Dakota laid it on the couch. "Mom, call the police! The thieves live three houses down from us. And they might have the other artifacts there."

Afton hugged him and said, "You're safe!" She was crying tears of joy. "Thank God!"

Abigail called the police and told them that her son found the David Inscription. "Yes, the real artifact!" she said. "No, this is not a prank call. . . . Yes. . . . No. . . . Someone was there at the house, maybe one of the thieves, we don't know. . . . No, he found it at that house, but now we have it at our house. . . . Our address is . . ." When she hung up, she said, "They're coming."

• • •

Drying his curly black hair, Eeman walked out of the bathroom and over to the dining table. He saw the money he had left on the table and yelled, "Where's my pizza?" He looked around for it and shouted, "Why are there gardening tools in the living room? Why is the front door open?"

Then he looked at the open crate. "What?" He dug around inside it and tipped it over, convinced something was inside. There was nothing but bubble wrap.

Panicking, he called Ahmed. "Did you finish getting the artifacts down to the boat?"

"Nooo. I had one more. The David Inscription."

"Oh no. Start the boat! The pizza guy stole it!"

"You ordered a pizza?"

"Yeah, for the boat ride. You know I hate to cook. And the guy didn't even leave the pizza—and I'm starving! But then a gardener showed up and left his tools in the living room. I'm super confused. But the David Inscription is gone. And if one of those guys reports it to the police, they're going to be here faster than a toupee flies in a hurricane!

"Wow, Eeman. I don't even know what . . . Radomir's going to be furious! Get down to the boat! Avner and I are ready to leave."

Eeman ran outside, hopped into the delivery truck, and raced to **the marina**. He parked and ran down the dock to Radomir's yacht.

Ahmed had the engines running and the boat unmoored. Eeman leaped onto it, and Ahmed said, "We're out of here!" He steered the boat around the corner of the marina's **breakwater**, aimed it west, and pushed the throttle to full speed. He glared

at Eeman. "I can't believe you let a pizza guy steal the David Inscription. . . . No, I can believe it! You better take the blame for this. This wasn't my fault."

"I'll take the blame."

"You better."

After Ahmed calmed down, he turned around and saw Eeman sitting on a couch staring off at the sea. "Why don't you go down and say 'hi' to Avner. He's lying in one of the secret compartments."

"How long does he have to do that?"

"Until we're out of Israeli water."

Chapter 20
Wednesday afternoon, June 15, Herzliya.

In response to Abigail's phone call, two police officers showed up at the Knoxes' house. She opened the door. "Thanks for coming so quickly! I'm sure you heard about the artifacts that were stolen from the Israel Museum."

"We heard."

"Well, it's a long story, but my sons and a couple of neighbor friends began their own investigation into the matter, and they found the David Inscription a few houses down."

"Officers are checking out that house right now. Do you have the artifact here?"

"We do. Come in."

"These are my sons, Dakota and Hank," Abigail said. "These are their friends, our next-door neighbors, Afton and Ethan."

"Good to meet you all," an officer said. "Can we see the

artifact?"

Dakota brought them over to the couch and showed it to them.

"That's it!" one of the officers said.

"Wow!" the other officer exclaimed. "Great work, you guys! Can we sit down and talk about how you've come to have this in your possession?"

"Sure," Dakota said.

For the next twenty minutes, Dakota, Hank, and the Hansleys answered questions. As they talked to the officers, a man and a woman from the Israel Antiquities Authority showed up, placed the artifact in a padded box, and took it away.

When the police determined the house down the street was clear, the officers asked Dakota to walk there with them. The house was taped off with police tape and had several patrol cars out front.

The officers asked Dakota to describe where he had been in the house and what he had seen and heard. When they were done, they walked Dakota back to his house. Abigail and Afton stood on the porch waiting for him.

"We're all done for now," an officer said to Abigail. "A detective will follow up with you guys in the coming days. But until the criminals are caught, we'll be providing your family with police protection here at your house 24 hours a day."

"Oh, thank you! That makes me feel better," Abigail said.

Dakota agreed. "Thank you, officers."

"No. Thank *you!* The entire country of Israel thanks you."

A couple of hours later, Abigail's phone rang. It was Police Chief Mordecai Weisner. Abigail put him on speaker. He asked if the Knoxes would be willing to drive to the museum and if

Dakota could be part of a 7:00 p.m. news conference.

William, who had come home from work, said, "I think we can do that. Are you up for that, Dak?"

"I'm up for it."

Abigail told the chief, "I guess we'll do it!"

"Wonderful! This is going to be a huge story! Expect lots of reporters to be there with cameras and lights. I'll announce the exciting discovery and fill in the public with some of the important details. If he'd be willing, I'd love for Dakota to be available for a few questions during the event."

"I can do that," Dakota said.

"Excellent. Well, Knoxes, word has made it out to the press. They will be at the museum in droves, excited to meet you, Dakota, and give their viewers a feel-good story. Our whole country is going to be delighted with this! If you could be at the museum at 6:00 p.m., that would be great. Dakota, one of our detectives will brief you ahead of time with what you should avoid saying during the event. For example, you won't want to give away any personal details or names. And he'll sit with you during the conference in case you have any questions or need advice."

"Sounds good," Dakota said.

"We'll be there at 6:00!" Abigail said.

• • •

The Knoxes and Hansleys showed up at the Israel Museum a few minutes before 6:00 p.m. Detective Seth Geller introduced himself to the families and said, "Dakota, why don't we sit down over here and talk for a few minutes about the press conference. Your parents are welcome to join us."

When they sat down, the detective said, "Dakota, we're thrilled about the return of the David Inscription. This press conference is an opportunity to let people know that it's been found. Please feel free to answer the questions as forthrightly as you'd like. I encourage you, though, to keep your answers concise and free from details about where you're staying, why you're here for the summer, where your dad works, and things like that. Don't mention the names of your siblings. We want to keep you and your family safe."

"Okay, that sounds good," Dakota said.

An older man dressed in a dark navy-blue suit with a light blue police uniform shirt walked over. "Good evening, Knox family. I'm Police Chief Mordecai Weisner. You must be Dakota."

"Yes!"

"Thank you for agreeing to this."

"No problem."

"Detective Geller will sit with you during the press conference. Breina Becker from the Israel News Network will ask you a few questions. I asked her to keep it short and to go easy on you. You're going to do great."

"Thanks," Dakota said.

At 7:00 p.m., Mordecai Weisner, Seth Geller, and Dakota walked out of the museum. Mordecai went to the wood podium. Seth and Dakota sat at a table to his left. In front of them were dozens of news cameras, lights, and reporters. The David Inscription was propped up inside a clear plastic box in front of the podium.

"Good evening. I'm Israel's Chief of Police. My name is

Mordecai Weisner. I stood at this podium on June 8 to brief you on the theft of five artifacts from the Israel Museum. I assured you that we would work hard until they were all recovered. Well, I'm happy to report this evening that one of the artifacts, the David Inscription, was recovered today. The young man to my left, Dakota Knox, found it in Herzliya!"

The reporters and others attending the conference gave Dakota a standing ovation.

Abigail and Afton were teary-eyed as they looked at Dakota sitting there, humbly giving a quick point upward to signal that he wanted God to get the credit.

When the applause ended, Mordecai said, "The discovery of this artifact was a huge break in the case. . . . And the Israel Police Force will continue our investigation until the criminals are arrested and the other artifacts are returned to the museum. But I'm excited for you to meet the one behind today's recovery. Rather than him doing 50 interviews today, Breina Becker, from INN, was chosen to ask him a few questions. So Miss Becker, would you please join us?"

A woman in her thirties with long brown hair stepped up to a microphone. "Thank you, Chief Weisner. Dakota, thank you for taking the time to come to Jerusalem and allowing us to meet you. We are all thrilled about the artifact's recovery! First, why don't you tell us a little about yourself."

"My name is Dakota Knox. I'm from California and visiting Israel for the summer with my family. We love your country. We are followers of Jesus, and we love the Jewish people and the Biblical history that transpired here. We've had an amazing time exploring the country."

"I'm happy to hear that. How were you able to track the criminals to the house in Herzliya?"

Dakota looked at Hank, who had taped the GPS tracker to Avner's car, and smiled. He told Breina, "I can't reveal how we did that."

"Okay. I understand. What were you doing in the neighborhood where the artifact was found?"

"Well, I thought I had a good lead on the people involved with the heist. I thought I'd visit their house pretending to be

looking for yard work to earn money. The person inside was in the shower and yelled for me to come into the house. He thought I was a pizza delivery guy. I walked in and saw a crate with a label on it that indicated it had been shipped to the museum in Jerusalem. I opened it, and there it was. Well, it was wrapped in bubble wrap. I peeled it off, and to my amazement, I was holding the David Inscription!"

"Did you see the person who was in the home?"

"No."

"Do you think the other missing artifacts might have been in the house?"

"I don't know. Police officers arrived at the house pretty fast, and they didn't find any."

"Had you thought of calling the police and having *them* knock on the door?"

"Well, I love and appreciate the police, but I had already called them and reported what I knew on their tip line, and no one called me back."

The police chief looked uncomfortable with Dakota's comment.

"I also reported what I knew to Gershom Haddad, the chief of security at the museum, and he never returned my call. So I decided to conduct my own investigation with the help of my brother and a couple of close friends."

Dakota looked over at Afton and smiled.

"Were you afraid when you knocked on the door of the house?" Breina asked.

"Well, I was pretty nervous as I walked toward the house, but I prayed for courage, and I believe God gave me the courage I needed."

"What did you do when you had the artifact in your hands?"

"Ran for my life!"

Several reporters laughed.

"The courage was gone?" Breina asked, trying to be funny.

"No. I'd say that God also dispensed a bit of wisdom."

There was more laughter.

Breina asked, "Where did you run?"

Dakota smiled. Knowing he could not tell them where he ran and feeling a little playful, he half-talked and half-sang, "I ran, Breina. I ran so far away; I just ran; I ran all night and day. I couldn't get away."

Many in the crowd, familiar with the famous song by A Flock of Seagulls, bust out laughing, including the police chief.

Breina Becker looked confused and said, "But you *got* away."

"I know. I was just joking a bit."

Breina smiled. "I guess that went over my head. But in all seriousness, Dakota, where did you run?"

Dakota looked at Detective Geller for help.

The detective leaned toward the mic and said, "Dakota won't be answering that question."

Breina asked, "When you were on your way to Israel, did you ever envision yourself being caught up in a heist?"

"No. That wasn't on our itinerary." There were more chuckles from the reporters. "I came here to surf and explore the country, enjoy the summer with my family."

"You like to surf?" Breina asked.

"Yes, I like to surf at Herzliya. The waves have been really good."

"What are your plans for the future?"

"Well, I'm starting college in September, studying criminal justice. I'd like to work for the Department of Homeland Security someday. But for now, I'd like to enjoy the rest of the summer. I'll probably go surfing in the morning."

"Well, thank you, Dakota, for allowing us to get to know you a little better. Israel and the Jewish people thank you for your help recovering the David Inscription, and we hope you and your family enjoy the rest of your stay here."

"You're welcome," Dakota said. "Thanks for having me."

Chapter 21
Wednesday, June 15, Mediterranean Sea, 6:30 p.m.

As Detective Geller prepped Dakota for the 7:00 p.m. press conference, Radomir's yacht raced west across the Mediterranean Sea. It was a long modern-looking white yacht. Its three levels included beds for twenty people, an outdoor hot tub, a spacious living room, kitchen, an elegant dining room, and several comfortable outdoor seats.

Eeman was in the kitchen microwaving a frozen pizza. Avner had come out of hiding and was relaxing on a couch in the living room. Ahmed was at the helm dreading the phone call to Radomir that he knew he had to make. He picked up his phone and dialed Radomir's number.

Radomir answered. "How's **Poseidon's Dream** doing?"

"Your boat's fine, Boss. How are you?"

"Cut to the point. I can tell you have bad news."

"Well, yes, I do have a bit of bad news, but I also have some good news. Would you like the good news first?"

"How long have you worked for me, Ahmed?"

"Right. Always the good news first. Well, the good news is that Eeman, Avner, and I are on the yacht and sailing to England with the artifacts safely hidden away on the boat . . . uh, except for one."

"Except for one?"

"Yeah, that's the bad news."

"You know I hate bad news."

"Well, Eeman was showering around lunchtime today, and a pizza delivery guy walked into the house and stole the David Inscription."

"Are you kidding me?" Radomir unleashed several vulgarities about Eeman's incompetence and history of failures and said, "Put him on the phone for me!"

Ahmed handed his phone to Eeman.

"Eeman! I'd put a bullet through your head if I were there," Radomir said. "But I'm not. I'm tempted to tell Ahmed to toss

you overboard and feed you to the sharks!"

"I'm sorry, Boss."

"I don't want your apology; I want my money back. I'd make Avner return the $500,000, but he did his part. You're the one who lost it. So here's what we're going to do. I'm cutting your salary in half until you pay it off."

"I understand, Boss. Half pay is very gracious of you. Happy to be alive, sir."

"Put Ahmed back on."

Eeman handed the phone back to Ahmed.

Radomir asked him, "When will you guys be back in England?"

"I haven't had time to calculate that because we left in such a rush."

"Let me know when you figure it out."

"I will. Hey Boss, we're watching Israel News Network. You might turn it on. Israel's police chief is going to do a press conference regarding the David Inscription."

"I'll turn it on. We'll talk later."

• • •

Radomir hung up and turned on INN. The police chief was explaining the recovery of the David Inscription. When the TV camera zoomed in on the artifact, Radomir screamed at the TV, "That's mine!"

When the conference was over, Radomir called an old acquaintance in Israel.

"Tarkyn, this is Radomir Lucic."

"Rado! It's been a year or two. How are you?"

"I've been better. I need you to take someone out. You still working?"

"Of course."

"What are you charging these days for someone in Israel?"

"For a repeat customer, 50,000 U.S. dollars in bitcoin."

"Your prices go up every year, don't they?"

"Well, if you want the best."

"I do."

"Who do you want dead?"

"His name is Dakota Knox. He broke into a house we were renting and stole one of my artifacts that I paid $500,000 for."

"Horrible. Where can I find him?"

"I'm pretty confident he lives in Herzliya. I heard him say tonight that the waves have been good and that he's looking forward to surfing tomorrow morning. So try Herzliya beach. I'll send you his picture in a couple of minutes."

"I normally ask for a deposit upfront, Radomir, but I know you're good for it."

"Of course. I'll send you full payment as soon as you take him out."

"Sounds good. I'll let you know when he's dead."

Chapter 22
Thursday morning, June 16, Herzliya.

Dakota walked downstairs the following day and was delighted to see that his mom had made **French toast** for breakfast.

"Thanks, Mom. Wow. What a day yesterday! It seems like a dream."

"It does seem like a dream. You handled yourself so well during the press conference. Your dad and I are so proud of you!"

"Thanks."

She came up behind him and kissed the back of his head. "You're a hero, Dakota. Video clips of the press conference are

on every news website I checked. Jerusalem Post. Daily Caller. Fox. Epoch. Newsmax."

Jalynn gave Dakota a high five. "You're famous, Dak! And that Flock of Seagulls bit cracked me up!"

"I thought you'd like that, Jay."

"Your grandparents, aunts, and uncles are calling and texting," Abigail said. "They can't believe you were on the news."

Dakota held up his phone. "I have about 50 texts this morning from friends. I haven't even read a fourth of them. I just want to go surfing and chill today."

"I understand, and you should," his mom said. "That was an emotionally draining day. But there's one person who wants to meet with you today that I think you should agree to meet."

"No way. I'm spent."

"Nathaniel Efron, the Prime Minister of Israel."

"Seriously?"

"Seriously. He asked if our family and the Hansleys could come to Balfour at 3:00 p.m."

"Balfour?"

"It's like the White House, but it's the official residence for Israel's Prime Ministers. It's officially called Beit Aghion. But it's commonly called Balfour, after the name of the street that it's on. Might you be up for that?"

"Sure."

"Good, because your dad and I already said yes. So did Steven and Nicola."

"Anything for you, Mom."

"Anything for you, Dak."

He chuckled.

"Enjoy your French toast," she said.

"I will, thanks, but then I'm going surfing. It will be good for my soul to enjoy God's creation for a while."

When Dakota finished eating and reading his Bible, he texted Afton:

> Good morning! What a day yesterday. Thanks for your help and support. I hear that we're going to Balfour today to meet the Prime Minister. How crazy is that?
>
> **Afton:** Yeah, Balfour at 3:00 p.m. Super crazy!
>
> **Dakota:** I'm going surfing. Want to go?
>
> **Afton:** Oh, thanks for the invite. I'm too tired to go out in the water this morning. I'll sit on the deck and watch you, though!

Dakota smiled. He hadn't told anyone yet, but he loved Afton. And knowing that she would be watching him brought joy to his heart.

He went into the backyard, grabbed his board, and applied some fresh wax to it. He stretched for a couple of minutes and then walked down the path to the sand and paddled out. The water didn't have its typical blue hue. The lingering marine layer along the coast gave the water a dark greenish appearance. A slight onshore breeze made the surfing conditions less than ideal, but that kept the crowd away. Dakota was happy to have the waves to himself. He caught a wave, did a few turns, and paddled back out. He noticed a strong current pulling him to the north.

When Dakota sat up on his board, he saw a splash about 20 feet in front of him to the west. Half a second later, he heard what sounded like a gun go off behind him, to his right, somewhere on the cliffs north of their neighborhood. A couple of seconds later, there was another splash about ten feet away, followed by the sound of another gunshot. Dakota realized that someone with a high-powered rifle was shooting at him. *What in the world? This is crazy!* He quickly rolled off his board and tried to sink as deep as he could. He heard the third bullet hit his board. *Avner or whoever he's working with must be trying to kill me. What do I do? I have no cover. He'll wait for me to surface. I can't swim south, away from the gunman. The current is too strong.*

Dakota undid the leash around his ankle, swam underwater about 30 yards away from the board, and popped up for a quick breath. He heard the gun go off but didn't see where the bullet went. He swam in a different direction about six feet underwater, hoping the shooter couldn't see him. He came up for a breath. Two more shots. *I can't do this very long. He'll eventually get me. God, please help me.*

• • •

Afton set her coffee down when she heard the gunshots. They were coming from the bluff just north of her house. She looked to the north, but another house blocked the view of the cliffs. She peered out at the sea, looking for Dakota. *Where is he? There's his board, but why isn't he on his board?*

She grabbed the binoculars off the table. Looking through them, she saw Dakota's head pop up for a second, then go

162

down, followed by two splashes nearby that coincided with the gunshots. *Oh my goodness! Someone's shooting at Dakota!*

She ran downstairs, yelling, "I need the keys, Dakota's in trouble! Someone's shooting at him from the cliffs."

Dakota's mom, who was over for coffee with Nicola, said, "Oh my God! I'm blocking Nicola's car. Take mine." She tossed her keys to Afton.

"Afton, let's just call the police . . ." her mom yelled.

Afton was already out the door. She jumped in the Bronco, started the engine, and peeled out in reverse down the driveway. *Oh God, keep Dakota safe!* At the bottom of the driveway, she skidded to a stop, shifted the car into drive, and pushed the gas pedal to the floor.

The 330-horsepower, twin-turbo V-6 engine pushed Afton back into the seat. A police officer who'd been assigned to help protect the families was dozing in his patrol car in front of the Knoxes' house. As Afton sped away, she shoved her palm into the Bronco's horn and purposely clipped the side mirror of his car. *That should wake him up!*

• • •

After Afton dashed out the door, Nicola called the police.

Abigail darted outside to get the attention of the police officer. She yelled at him through his window. "Someone's shooting at my son in the water."

He rolled down his window and said, "I think he just drove by and clipped my car."

"No, that was a 17-year-old girl going to help my son, Dakota."

"Do you know where the shots are coming from?"

"They sound like they're coming from the bluff just north of here."

"I'm on it!"

He did a U-turn and sped off.

• • •

Dakota swam for his life. He held his breath for as long as he could, then came up in different spots for quick breaths. After a few minutes of this, Dakota was exhausted. But he had an idea. He remembered that his surfboard had been constructed with unique materials that made it "practically bulletproof."

If I can swim to my board underwater, I can grab the leash and pull the board to the shore. Then I can hold up the board as a shield and run for cover. It's worth trying because if the gunman hits me out here in the water, I'll drown.

He began swimming underwater back toward his board. It was about 50 yards away. As he swam, the song "Swim Good" by Switchfoot came into his mind. *I'm about to try to swim from something bigger than me. Kick off my shoes and swim good, swim good.*

He looked up and saw his board floating on the surface of the water. Nearly out of breath, he found the end of his leash and wrapped it around his left ankle. He surfaced, blew the air out of his lungs, and sucked in a deep breath. A bullet whizzed past him. He went back under and started swimming toward the shore. *God, help me to swim good!*

Dakota swam, dragging the board behind him. Even a couple of feet below the surface, he could hear more gunshots. When he reached shallow waist-deep whitewash near the shore, he swam under his board, grabbed it from underneath, and stood, holding it as a shield. Two shots immediately hit it, knocking Dakota back a couple of feet. *But I'm alive! The board worked.*

Keeping the board angled toward the gunshots, he darted out of the water toward the bluff for cover. The gunman fired seven more shots. Three hit the surfboard. As he ran, Dakota realized his board would only be bulletproof for so long—the material was compromised. More hits in the same vicinity would surely puncture it.

If I can make it to that cement fire ring, I can hide behind it for cover and wait for help. He ran as fast as he could. He had thirty more yards, but the sand was deep, and his strength was spent. The next shot hit his board by his left hand, instantly ripping the board from his grip. It fell to the sand. His shield was down. The gunman discharged two more shots. Both misses. Ten more yards. *I don't know if I'm going to make it.* Five yards. Dakota collapsed behind the fire ring's cement wall. He laid the side of his face in the sand and gasped for oxygen. Two more shots hit the cement.

How long can I lie here? Is the gunman going to come down on the beach now? Does anyone hear the gunshots? Will anyone come to help me? Lord, God, in Jesus's name, You've got to help me. Someone's trying to kill me. Send help.

• • •

Afton raced the Bronco down the street and barely slowed down to make the right turn to the beach. She sped down the emergency vehicle access road, crashed through a barricade, and bounced over some bumps. The SUV was on the sand, and she floored it. The song "Now" by Paramore was playing on the radio: "There's a time and place to die, but this ain't it. . . . If there's a future, we want it."

Well, this is an appropriate song! Afton thought.

She angled the Bronco northwest toward the water, where there was harder sand and a faster path to Dakota. She could barely see him about 500 yards to the north lying on the beach. *How did you get out of the water with someone shooting at you? Have you been hit? Hold on, Dakota. Help is coming!*

• • •

After Dakota prayed, he looked down the beach. *Is that a car coming?* It was, and he recognized the grill—it was the red Bronco with its headlights on racing along the water's edge. It was a good 300 yards south of him, but it was coming fast. *Thank You, God!*

• • •

A bullet smashed into the windshield of the Bronco. Afton screamed. She could feel tiny bits of glass hit her face. *Good Lord! Now he's shooting at me. Protect me, God!* She started swerving the car in an S-pattern to make it harder to hit. The gunman still managed to hit it. Ding. Pop. Crack. The windshield had two more holes in it. She kept the gas pedal pressed to the floor.

About 50 yards away from Dakota, she angled the four-wheel-drive SUV toward the fire ring, then whipped it counterclockwise around it to put a barrier between Dakota and the gunman. She opened her door, jumped out, hopped over the fire ring, and said, "Dakota, it's me. I'm getting you out of here."

"Afton! Thank you!"

"Are you hurt?"

"I'm okay."

She reached out her hand to help him up and said, "Stay down and crawl in the back seat."

Afton jumped in the front. Four more shots hit the passenger side of the Bronco.

When she grabbed the steering wheel, she saw her hand. It had blood from Dakota's hand on it. "You *are* hurt!" she said.

Dakota settled into the back seat. "I'm all right. Go, go!"

"Hold on," Afton said as she stepped on the gas. The Bronco kicked up some sand and took off. She cranked the steering wheel and headed south, away from the gunman. Dakota's battered surfboard, still connected to his ankle, was whipping around in the air next to the car. The gunman's next shot shattered the back window. The following one blew out the rear tire on the driver's side. Afton kept driving.

When they were out of the gun's range, Dakota sat up and leaned forward over the center console. He looked at Afton and said, "I prayed God would send someone to help me, and I looked up, and there you were. Thank you! Someone was trying to kill me."

"Ya think?"

He laughed. "I think so!"

"You saved my life, Afton! Seriously. Look at the windshield! He could have killed you." Dakota got choked up. "You were willing to lay down your life to save mine. Thank you!"

"Didn't Jesus say something about that?"

"He did."

She turned left on the sand and drove up the paved access road.

"What's that banging noise?" Dakota asked.

"Well, it's either the rim of the blown tire or your surfboard that's still attached to your ankle."

"My surfboard?"

"You didn't take your leash off, and your board is dragging outside."

"Oops."

Dakota opened the door and pulled the battered board inside. As he did, he noticed that his left hand was bleeding. He looked at it more closely. The bullet hadn't hit his hand, but it was close enough to send shards of surfboard resin into his skin and cause some bleeding. He applied pressure to it with his right hand to stop the blood flow.

"I think I'm going to need a new board."

"I'd say so!"

At the top of the hill, Afton stopped the car, turned around, and looked at Dakota. "How's your hand? Should I take you to urgent care?"

"No, it's just got a few cuts on it. I'll clean it at home."

"Can I see it?"

He held it up for her. As she was examining the cuts, he marveled at her bravery, compassion, and beauty. He thought, *Afton, you are the most beautiful girl I've ever seen, inside and out!*

Afton slowly gave him his hand back and said, "I think

with some soap and water and Neosporin, you'll be okay." She looked up and down the street. "I'm not sure if we should head home." She picked up her phone to call her mom but saw a text from Dakota's mom.

> **Abigail:** We saw what you did, Afton, rescuing Dakota. Oh, my goodness!!! We love you! Thank you! It's safe for you guys to come home. More police have arrived.

> **Afton:** Anytime :) We're coming home.

She set her phone down and told Dakota, "We can head home. Your mom said it's safe."

Afton drove the dinged-up Bronco slowly up the street. As they got closer to home, they saw their moms and siblings in the road waiting for them, waving. Next to them were three police officers, two patrol cars, and several curious neighbors. Afton pulled the car up and turned it off. Afton and Dakota opened their doors and were smothered with hugs and kisses from every direction.

Dakota got emotional, hugged his mom, and laid his head on her shoulder, crying. "Mom, they almost killed me. I almost drowned." He couldn't say anything else.

She hugged him and cried. "I'm so glad you're okay, Dakota. Afton saved your life. We saw what she did from the house."

"I know, she did. God sent her just in time."

A call came in on a policeman's radio. The voice said, "We captured the gunman. He's in cuffs in our car. I was having a hard time finding him holed up in the cliffs. But a kid flying a **drone** with a camera on it followed me and told me where the

guy was hiding. Anyway, we got him!"

"Great work! Give that kid a medal," the officer responded. He announced the good news to the crowd outside the Knoxes' house. "The gunman has been captured! We got him."

Several people clapped. The Knoxes and Hansleys looked at each other, and Nicola said, "A kid with a drone? Ethan? . . . No, he's right here."

"Where's Hank?" Abigail asked.

"I haven't seen him for a while," Jalynn said.

An officer pointed at a kid walking toward them. "Is that him?"

They turned to look. Hank was walking down the middle of the street, holding his drone in his left hand and the remote controller in his right. When Hank saw Dakota standing there, he took off running straight for him. He laid the drone down and gave him a big hug.

"I thought that man was going to kill you. I grabbed my drone and tried to help." Hank started crying. "I'm so glad you're alive, D."

Dakota looked into his brown eyes. "You did help, Hank! The police officer said you helped him find the gunman. Thank you!"

Hank turned to Afton next. "Thank you, Afton, for saving my brother's life. I watched you drive down the beach while the man was shooting at you. You're our hero." He wiped away his tears and hugged her.

"You're welcome, Hank. Thanks for helping the police! *You're* my hero."

There wasn't a dry eye in the Knox or Hansley family.

Abigail said, "Let's head inside. The police can join us. I'm sure they need to ask you guys a few questions. And I need to call your father and let him know what happened."

Chapter 23
Thursday afternoon, June 16, Herzliya.

An hour after the police officers finished filing their report, Abigail received a phone call from the Prime Minister's secretary. She said Nathaniel Efron heard about the shooting and wanted to reschedule the meeting at Balfour to the following day at 3:00 p.m. "Dakota's been through enough today. Prime Minister Efron would like for him to take it easy and tend to his injured hand."

"Yes. That would be good," Abigail said. "Thank Mr. Efron for being sensitive to that. Tomorrow will work fine."

Dakota was lying on the couch, nodding his head in agreement.

The secretary continued. "We will have two limousines pick you and the Hansley family up at 1:30 p.m. And a police escort will accompany you here."

"Wonderful. Thank you for having us. We'll be ready."

"The Prime Minister and our entire office send Dakota and your family our good wishes, and we look forward to meeting you all tomorrow."

Abigail hung up and looked at William, who had come home from work. "Well, that's a relief! The Prime Minister heard about the shooting and wants to postpone the meeting until tomorrow."

"That's great news," William said.

Abigail looked over at Dakota. "What can I get for you, Dakota? Are you hungry?"

"Yes, please. A sandwich would be amazing."

"You're getting the best sandwich you've ever had! I'm so thankful you're alive."

While Abigail was making sandwiches, Afton's mom Nicola came over. "How's Dakota?"

"He's doing okay."

Dakota heard his mom's response and said, "I'm fine! I might not be able to surf for a few days, but I'm good. How's Afton doing?"

"She's napping. I think she's pretty shaken up. *I'm* shaken up."

Abigail set down a head of lettuce, nodded in sympathetic agreement, and gave Nicola a hug.

Dakota was saddened to hear Afton was shaken up. He silently lifted up a prayer for her. *God, I pray for my friend Afton. You saw what she did today. That must have been scary. Thank You for her! Bless her with a good nap. Comfort her heart. Give her peace and a sense of Your presence. In Jesus's name, I pray. Amen.*

Dakota heard Nicola tell his mom, "Steven and I were

173

talking, and I have an idea I want to run by you. We've decided that the kids and I will go back to England for a couple of weeks while law enforcement tracks down this crime ring. We think it's too dangerous to justify the kids and me staying in Israel."

Dakota sat up. *Afton's leaving?*

Nicola continued. "And here's our idea. We want you and the kids to come with us. We love you guys. It would be so fun to show you around England. Will you guys think about coming?"

"Wow, Nicola. We *will* think about it. That sounds amazing. We've never been to England. We'd love to spend time there with you all. I'll talk to William and the kids about it."

Dakota spoke up. "Yes—I say yes!"

"If that's where Evelyn's going, I'm going!" Jalynn said.

Abigail smiled. "Well, there's a couple of votes in favor of it!"

. . .

That evening, Abigail ran the idea by William. He agreed that it sounded like a prudent plan.

"Well, then, we'll do it," Abigail said.

"Where will you guys stay?" William asked.

"Nicola said they live in Marylebone, a district of London. It looks nice. So, I just thought we'd rent a VRBO or Airbnb close to their house rather than a hotel."

"Wonderful, Babe. Do it!"

"We might come back after a week or two, depending on what's happening here. With Dakota's discovery, maybe the police will be able to track down the thieves. I pray for that."

"I do, too."

· · ·

After dinner, Dakota went into the backyard, looking for a quiet place to sit and reflect on the day. He settled into a chair next to one of the poolside fires. He put his feet up, listened to the waterfall, and admired the pink and orange swirls in the clouds. Dakota closed his eyes and prayed. *Heavenly Father, thank You for this day, for Your grace and mercy. I know I've been given everlasting life and that death for the Christian is the doorway to glory and eternal joy in Your presence. I don't fear dying. I know I will go straight to Heaven because of Jesus's death on the cross for my sins. But, God, I'm thankful to be alive. I don't think You're done with me here. You kept me alive out in the water and on the beach. You truly are my good Shepherd. Thank You.*

He sat by the fire for a few minutes thinking about the day, wondering what he might be doing if his family had not come to Israel or visited the museum. He also wondered how Afton was doing. *Is she up from her nap? Is she doing okay?* He texted her:

Hey Afton, how are you? Heard you were napping.

Afton: I'm up. I'm okay. I was just sitting and talking with my parents. How are you? What are you up to?

Dakota: I'm doing good. . . . thankful to be alive. I'm sitting by the fire in the backyard, enjoying the beautiful sunset.

Afton: That sounds relaxing.

Dakota: My mom is making acai bowls. Would you like one?

Afton: Sounds yum.

Dakota: Come on over!

Afton: I'll be there in a couple of minutes :)

A few minutes later, Afton walked over and sat in a chair next to Dakota. "It's really nice out right now. The sunset is amazing, and this fire and the pool. Beautiful."

Abigail walked outside. "Hi, Afton!" She set two **acai bowls** down on the small wooden table between their chairs. She bent over and hugged Afton. "Thanks again for helping Dakota today! I'm so glad you're both okay."

"Of course. Thank you for the acai bowl."

"You're the best, Mom! Thank you!"

Afton looked at the bandage wrapped around Dakota's left hand. "How's your hand doing?"

"It's okay. It doesn't hurt too bad. Thanks for saving me today!"

"You're welcome. I'm so grateful you're okay."

"How are *you*, Afton? You said just 'okay' in your text."

"I'm doing better after a good nap. That was a pretty terrifying experience today. When I went home this afternoon, my hands were shaking as I thought about the bullets smashing into the windshield. But look! My hands aren't shaking

anymore."

She held up her hands for him to observe.

"Oh good," he said.

"To be honest, Dakota, what I'm wrestling with now is in my mind."

"What's troubling you?"

"Well, I'm wondering why God would allow the shooting today. You love Him like no one I've ever met. You rescued this amazing, cherished artifact that verifies the existence of David, and then God allows someone to shoot at you? Why?" She wiped a tear away from her eye.

Dakota turned in his chair. "Thanks for sharing that with me, Afton. I don't know why God allows certain things to happen, but I stand on what I *do* know. His love for me, for you, is unchanging and everlasting. He's also promised to never leave me or forsake me. And He's promised to work all things together for good in the lives of those who love Him. Knowing that is enough for me."

"That's helpful, standing on what we *know* to be true rather than being tossed around in the waves of things we don't know."

"Yes! And I like the wave analogy."

"Well, now that I'm a surfer, you know, those illustrations come to me."

Dakota smiled. "You *are* a surfer!"

"But Dakota, couldn't God have stopped that gunman from coming after you?"

"For sure. But He's given humans free will, and most of the time, He allows people to do what's in their hearts. And someone wanted to kill me today. And that gunman exercised his freedom doing that. But with God's help—and yours!—I survived it."

"It makes me question if God should have given us free will to do whatever's in our hearts," Afton said. "That results in a lot of crime, bullying, stealing, adultery. It seems to me that maybe God shouldn't have created us with the freedom to do all those awful things."

Dakota said, "God could have created a world with creatures that were pre-programmed to always do what was good and pleasing to Him. But the relationships between the creatures and God would have all been void of love."

Afton thought about that, took a bite from the acai bowl, and asked, "Why's that?"

"Well, for meaningful, genuine, loving relationships to exist between God and people, people must be free—free to love Him or free to hate Him," Dakota said. "If there's no choice allowed or free will, love can't exist. So, God saw it worth it to grant humans real freedom. It allows love to exist between people and God and for love to happen between one person and another. Think about it this way. If your dad arranged a marriage for you and picked out your husband, and the guy's parents forced him to marry you, would you consider your husband's proposal and time with you to be an expression of genuine love?"

"Of course not," Afton said. "He had no choice."

"Right! Love can only happen when a person has the freedom to do otherwise. So God gave humans real freedom. Yes, it allows for a lot of bad to take place, but it also allows for love, the highest good to exist."

"Wow. I haven't thought about it that way, Dakota. It's good to talk to you about all of this. Thank you."

"Of course. You know, I mentioned a couple of minutes ago that God works all things together for good. I'm confident He's going to do that with this shooting today. Maybe the shooting will draw more attention to the significance of the David Inscription. Maybe God will use this for the furtherance of the gospel. I don't know."

Afton smiled and nodded. "That's a great perspective."

Dakota said, "Before you came over, I was wondering how different this day might have been had our family not come to Israel. And I thought, 'I probably wouldn't have been shot at today!' But then I was reminded that the David Inscription might have gone missing forever. I wouldn't have met you. And I wouldn't be sitting here enjoying this sunset. So, I just want to give God thanks in every situation and trust that He knows what's best."

Afton smiled and started to laugh. "I'm sorry. I just saw a meteor fly across the sky right behind you, and the colors of the sky, and you just mic-dropping all this beautiful truth. I'm blown away by the beauty of this moment. All right, you were saying—"

"I was just going to mention one last thing. God is working on us. Romans 8 says that God is seeking to conform us into the image of His Son, Jesus. One of the ways He chisels away at our character is through trials and adversity. Think of the people you've met who are like Jesus—loving, humble, compassionate, patient, kind. Aren't they beautiful?"

"For sure!"

"Well, it often takes adversity and trials to forge that kind of character."

"That's good, Dakota. Really helpful. Thank you. Earlier today, I wondered, 'What would have happened if *our* family hadn't come to Israel?' And I thought that you might have died on the beach today and . . ."

She stopped mid-sentence and looked up toward the stars. Her eyes were wet with emotion. "And that wrecked me, Dakota!" She couldn't hold in the emotion. Afton leaned forward, put her hands over her face, and cried.

Dakota put his hand on her back as he thought of what to say.

A minute later, Afton sat up and wiped her eyes. "Seriously, Dakota! I thanked God for bringing my family here. I really appreciate your friendship."

"I appreciate yours, too, Afton."

They sat there for a couple more hours, talking and looking at the stars. Around 11:30, Afton yawned. "I should head home."

"I'll walk you home."

"Thank you."

Dakota walked her around the wall and to the wood steps of the deck in their backyard. He walked up the steps and opened the door for her. She said, "Dakota, it's been such a wonderful evening. Thank you."

"I agree. I'm so glad you came over. Would you mind if I gave you a hug?" Dakota asked.

"I'd love a hug."

Dakota and Afton wrapped their arms tightly around each other, her head resting on his shoulder, his head leaned against hers. Dakota's words had already melted away most of Afton's anxious thoughts about the shooting. But his strong, warm embrace dispatched them all. In his arms, all she felt was joy, peace, and contentment. She closed her eyes and felt like she could stand there with him for hours.

"Thanks for spending time with me tonight, Dakota."

"Thanks for saving my life today."

"Of course. I'd do it again."

"Hopefully, you won't have to. But maybe I can repay you someday."

"This hug is repayment enough."

He slowly leaned back and looked Afton in the eyes.

She wondered, *Is he going to kiss me?*

He smiled and said, "We should get some rest. God bless you, Afton. Sleep well, and I'll see you tomorrow, okay?"

Everything in her wanted to say, *No. Don't go quite yet! Sit with me on the porch a little longer. Put your arm around me. I love you, Dakota Knox!* But she said, "Okay. Thanks for walking me home. God bless you. Sweet dreams. I'll see you tomorrow."

He turned and walked down the steps. As soon as he reached the bottom, he saw a meteorite shoot across the sky. He pointed at it and looked back at Afton. "Did you see that?"

"I did! It was spectacular!"

"Okay, goodnight!"

She stood there in the doorway and watched him walk the length of their backyard and disappear around the wall.

Chapter 24
Friday, June 17, Herzliya.

At 1:30 p.m. the following day, two limousines pulled up in front of the Knoxes' and Hansleys' homes.

Jalynn twirled out the front door, exclaiming, "First ride in a limo!"

As the Knoxes walked out the door, Hank said, "Hey Mom, Dad, can all the kids ride in one limo and the parents in the other?"

William looked at Abigail for her thoughts.

She said, "I'm fine with it." She lowered her voice and leaned toward William. "That doesn't sound like something Hank would ask."

Hank overheard and said, "Dakota told me to ask."

"Ah!" Abigail looked over at the Hansleys and saw Afton standing with her family. She had on a white dress and looked like a beautiful princess. "I think I know what's happening."

"What?" William asked.

"I think Dakota's in love." She walked over to Nicola and Steven and said, "I guess the kids want to ride together. Are

182

you guys okay with that?"

Nicola said, "Sure, if that's what they'd like."

"Dakota wants to sit next to Afton!" Hank said extra loudly.

"Hank!" Dakota said, "What are you talking about?"

Hank slapped Dakota on the back, "Couldn't resist, big bro. Everyone knows. It's obvious you like her!"

Dakota was embarrassed, mainly because the Hansleys heard every word.

The Knox and Hansley kids settled into their limousine.

"Wow!" Jalynn said, "These things are sweet!"

Ethan was amazed. "Look at all these sodas and snacks."

"I like your gray sports coat and tie, Dakota. Very nice," Afton said.

"Oh, thanks. I like your dress."

"Thank you! I thought I should dress up a little, visiting the Prime Minister."

Dakota agreed. "It seems like a good occasion to dress up."

Halfway to Balfour, Afton said, "I didn't find out about this until this morning, Dakota. But my parents want me, Ethan, and Evelyn to go back to London until the archaeology thief is caught."

"Yeah. I heard our moms talking about that yesterday."

"Would you guys want to come with us?" Afton asked.

"For sure! We'd all like to go. I'm just not sure how my dad feels about it. He and my mom were going to talk about it last night. I should text my mom and ask if they've made a decision."

> **Dakota:** Did you and Dad decide if we're going to London with the Hansleys?

Abigail: We're all talking about it right now. I'll get back to you in a little while.

Ten minutes later, Abigail texted Dakota back. He quietly read it, got a big smile, and said, "Guys, quiet. Good news from Mom!" He read it out loud:

Abigail: We're going to London with the Hansleys! We'll probably leave on Tuesday—four days from now.

There was a flurry of high fives and shouts:

"Woohoo!"

"Stoked!"

"Thank you, Mom and Dad!"

"England's going to be so fun!"

When they arrived at Balfour, an iron gate opened, and guards waved the limousines and police escort through. Dakota looked out the window at the large stone building and thought, *Wow! It doesn't look anything like the White House.*

As they got out of the limousines, they were cheered by some of the Balfour staff. The Prime Minister's secretary greeted them and ushered them inside and down a hallway toward Nathaniel Efron's office. As they passed by smiling staff, Dakota heard someone whisper, "That's the young man who found the stolen artifact." Another person said in a low voice, "He's the guy who survived the beach shooting."

Efron's secretary guided them to a door on the left side of the hallway, opened it, and said, "Prime Minister Efron, the Knox and Hansley families have arrived."

"Excellent. Please welcome them in."

"Knoxes and Hansleys, it is my pleasure to introduce you to the Prime Minister of Israel, Nathaniel Efron."

He stood, came out from behind his desk, and said, "Welcome! Please come in. What an honor to have all of you with us. Welcome to Beit Aghion. Thank you for making the drive and spending part of your afternoon with me."

He shook all their hands and said, "Please have a seat on the couches."

Dakota thought, *this is surreal!* He had seen Nathaniel Efron in the news and read about him. *And now I'm sitting in his office talking to him.*

The Prime Minister sat at his desk and said, "The recovery of the David Inscription, one of our national treasures, means so much to the Jewish people. Dakota, I read how you rescued it with the help of your siblings and neighbor friends. I commend you for your bravery! I'm sorry our police department didn't respond to your phone call. My administration is following up with them about that. They need to take every tip seriously. But your ingenuity and bravery tracking down the artifact is inspiring."

"Thank you, Prime Minister," Dakota said.

Nathaniel added, "We were horrified yesterday to hear of the assassination attempt on your life. We suspect it was related to the artifact theft and are investigating it from every possible angle. But Afton, your courage driving up the beach to rescue Dakota was heroic. It sounded like something out of a movie."

Afton smiled. "Thank you, Prime Minister."

"And Hank, I read about how you helped one of our police officers with your drone. That was very impressive! Our entire

nation breathed a sigh of relief when we found out the shooter was captured, and all of you were okay."

"Yes, so did we!" Afton's dad Steven said.

The **Prime Minister** continued. "I want to assure you all that detectives are working around the clock to apprehend the people involved with the theft of the artifacts and the shooting yesterday."

"Thank you, Prime Minister," Dakota said.

William Knox agreed. "We appreciate that, Prime Minister."

"Of course. Both of your families will always be friends of the Israeli people. To express our deep appreciation for your help recovering the artifact, we have something for you. As you may have heard, the Israeli government, the Museum, and some generous donors are offering up to 5,000,000 shekels in rewards for tips leading to the recovery of the stolen artifacts. So for the recovery of the David Inscription, it is my honor to present to your families some of that reward money."

From behind his desk, he pulled out two large checks for

1,000,000 shekels each. One was made out to the Hansley Family and the other to the Knox Family.

Steven Hansley said, "That's incredible—thank you so much."

"Wow!" William said, "That is very gracious."

Jalynn whispered to Abigail, "How much is one of those checks in American money?"

Abigail whispered, "Probably about $300,000. Isn't that nice of them?"

"Excuse me, Prime Minister," Dakota said. "That is very kind of you and the people of Israel to offer us the reward money, but we can't take it. Our family is here to help Israel with its laser defense system. We don't want to take anything from you all. I didn't try to find those stolen artifacts for money or fame or . . . I looked for the artifacts because they are important, and I believe God allowed me to stumble upon a clue. I wanted to be faithful to Him. So, Mom, Dad, I'm sorry. Prime Minister, thank you for offering us the reward, but we can't receive that money."

When Dakota finished, the only sound that could be heard was the low hum of the air conditioner. Everyone in the room looked at him, some in shock, some in disbelief, and some with admiration.

Afton broke the silence. "Same for the Hansleys, Prime Minister! Our families are already so blessed. We'd rather the money stay here in Israel. Right, Mom and Dad?"

Ethan's head fell backward on the couch as he pretended to faint with disappointment.

As her parents whispered to one another, the Prime Minister said, "I don't know what to say, except, thank you, on behalf of all Israelis. And thank you, Knox and Hansley parents, for raising these fine kids. I'd insist that you take the money, but I sense the sincerity in your voices, so I will honor your request if your parents are agreeable to it."

They all agreed.

"Very well then, we will put the money to good use elsewhere. Maybe it can be used to help track down the other artifacts or invested in the ongoing search for new ones."

"That sounds good," Dakota said.

"But I do have one more gift," the Prime Minister said. "This one is specifically for you, Dakota. And I do *insist* you receive it!" He stood, walked over to his closet, and pulled out a brand-new surfboard. "We picked it up today at a local surf shop. They said it's the same size and shape as yours, but without the bulletproof materials. But Dakota, we are all praying that you will never need a bulletproof board again!"

Dakota checked it out. "Wow, a **Channel Islands surfboard**! This is a killer board. Thank you! I *will* receive it."

"Dakota, please don't use that word," Abigail said.

"What word?"

"*Killer*. I know it's slang but—"

"Yeah, probably not the best word."

The Prime Minister spent another twenty minutes talking with them and getting to know them before walking them out to the limousines and waving goodbye.

On the drive back to Herzliya, Dakota said,

188

"That was so cool! But you know what's cooler? We're all going to London!"

All of them agreed with high fives.

"That's going to be fun," Dakota said. "We've never been to England. Will you guys show us around?"

"Absolutely!" Afton said.

"What is there to do there?" Dakota asked.

"Well," Afton said, "you should bring your new surfboard."

"Serious? There are waves in London?"

Afton laughed. "No. The River Thames isn't known for its waves. But there *are* fun waves in Brighton, about a 55-mile drive from where we live."

"And now that you know how to surf," Dakota said, "you'll paddle out with me?"

"You know I will!" Afton smiled. "But I'll need to get a board."

"We'll find you one."

"Perfect. These guys probably won't want to go with us, but there are lots of good coffee shops in London."

Hank chimed in. "Yeah, we'll pass on those. Are there good restaurants?"

"Yes! All over. Everything you can imagine. Korean, Indian, Thai, Japanese. You name it, and we have it."

"Those are within walking distance of your house?" Hank asked.

"Yes!"

Hank pumped his fists. "I love London!"

"We could visit **Big Ben**," Afton said. "Buckingham Palace, where the Royal Family lives. Westminster Abbey, where Isaac Newton, George Handel, and other famous people are buried.

189

Saint James Park is super pretty. There's the Eye—an enormous Ferris wheel that gives you a breathtaking view of the city. We can ride around on the **double-decker buses**."

"The buses—that's what I want to do!" Jalynn said.

Afton gave her a side-hug. "Then we will, Jalynn! Oh, and Dakota, there's the British Museum! It's huge, and it's only a couple of kilometers from our house. We can walk or ride bikes there. They have a lot of artifacts that were discovered in Babylon, Assyria, and Egypt."

"Oh, yeah. I forgot about that. I'd love to visit it."

"The last time I went there was a few years ago," Afton said. "And, you know, those artifacts didn't interest me much at the time. But now, I would *love* to look at them!"

"Let's for sure do that," Dakota said. "I'll pass on the huge Ferris wheel thing. You know . . . the line is probably super long. And I wouldn't want to make you stand in . . ."

"Not to worry. I have a friend who works there. She'll let us right on."

"Oh."

Jalynn whispered to Afton, "He hates Ferris wheels. They're too high up."

Afton looked straight at him and said, "You're going!"

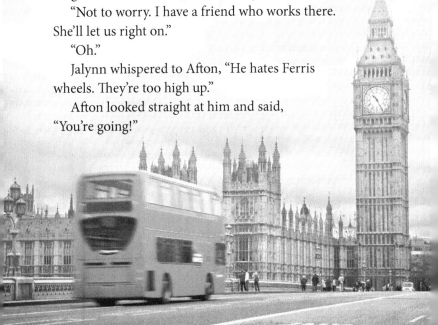

Chapter 25
Tuesday, June 21, Ben Gurion Airport, Israel.

Four days after their meeting with the Prime Minister, the Knoxes and Hansleys were off to **London**. Light Shield Defense Systems covered the cost of the flight and insisted the families fly first-class.

As they sat at their gate going over the seating arrangements, Hank said, "Let me guess, Dakota and Afton want to sit together."

Afton laughed. "No way, Hank. I'm sitting with you!"

"Really?"

"Yeah, I just hope you don't mind when I fall asleep and lean over on you."

"On second thought," Hank said, "you should probably sit with Dakota." Hank looked at Ethan. "You and me, buddy. No leaning over, though."

An hour into the flight and somewhere over the Mediterranean Sea, Afton turned from looking out the window and looked at Dakota. "I'm going to miss Israel and my dad. I hope we get to go back soon."

"So do I."

"Dakota, can I run something by you that I've been praying about?"

"Of course."

"I decided to change my college major."

"Really?"

"Yep."

"No more business management?"

"No. I want to study history and archaeology. I want to be an archaeologist."

"Wow! That's amazing, Afton."

"Yeah, I'm excited. But here's what I'm a little nervous to talk to you about."

"Don't be nervous."

"I'd like to study at a university with professors who have a Biblical worldview."

"I understand that desire."

"So here's my question. Would you be upset if I switched my college plans and attended Liberty University in the fall?"

"In Virginia?"

Afton nodded.

"Oh, my goodness!" Dakota said. "Seriously? That would be amazing!"

"Really?"

"Yes! It's a great school. I'd *love* for you to go there."

"Oh, I'm so relieved! You wouldn't be bothered by my being at the same campus as you?"

"Are you kidding me? No. I . . ."

Dakota paused. He almost said, "I *love* you, Afton!" but he had never told a girl that, and he didn't have the courage yet to say it. Thinking that Hank was probably trying to eavesdrop, Dakota lowered his voice. "Afton, to be transparent with you, I've gotten sad whenever I've thought about this summer coming to an end and that we weren't going to see each other anymore. But if you go to Liberty . . . Wow! We can continue hanging out."

Afton nodded in agreement, not knowing what to say, as tears formed in her eyes.

"Do you think your parents will allow you to move to the U.S. to attend Liberty?"

"Yes! I told them what I wanted to do, and they were amazingly supportive. So I'm excited! But I wouldn't switch to Liberty if it would bother you. Truth be told, Dakota, I've cried more than once thinking about the last day of summer and that we were going to have to say 'goodbye' and not see each other again."

Dakota looked surprised. "I didn't know you felt that way."

"I didn't know *you* felt that way," Afton said as she smiled and wiped a tear off her cheek.

"So we'll be together this fall after all," Dakota said. He marveled at how beautiful her green eyes looked with tears of joy in them. He opened his right hand and laid it palm side up on the center armrest.

Afton quickly placed her left hand in his. "Together!" she said.

Dakota looked at her hand in his, gripped it a bit tighter, and smiled at her. "I'm the happiest guy in the world right now."

"And I'm the happiest girl."

"I'm so thankful God caused our paths to cross."

"So am I, Dakota, so am I."

"Excuse me." A woman in her late fifties with short brown

hair knelt next to Dakota's seat. "I'm so sorry to interrupt. Would your name happen to be Dakota?"

"It is."

"Oh, good! I was pretty sure it was you. I watched your interview last week. I just want to thank you for your help recovering that artifact. That was very brave of you."

"Well, I give God all the credit and—"

"Are you heading home to California?"

"Not yet. We're going to England for a while."

"Oh yeah? What part?"

"London."

"How long?"

"Um . . . I'd rather not say."

"Oh, well, I'm sorry for being nosey," she said as she stood. "It was a pleasure to meet you in person, Dakota. Enjoy your time in London."

When the lady sat down a few rows behind them, Afton whispered to Dakota, "That was nice of her to stop by and say that."

"It was, but I don't want to tell a stranger how long I'm going to be somewhere."

"For sure. That was a little too personal."

A little while later, Dakota was reading a magazine article on things to see and do in London. "Afton, the Sherlock Holmes Museum is right by your house. That's so cool."

"It is! Have you read any of the Sherlock Holmes books?"

"A few, when I was younger. I loved them!"

"We'll go check it out, then!"

Dakota noticed a flight attendant walk by with a coffee in his hand. The woman who had stopped by his seat thanked the attendant for the drink and said, "I need to get online to send an email. I wasn't listening when the instructions were given. Could you help me, please?"

"Of course!"

When she was connected to the Internet, the flight attendant said, "Let me know if there's anything else I can get you, Mrs. Haddad."

Dakota looked up and squeezed Afton's hand as soon as he heard her last name. He leaned over and whispered in Afton's ear. "That lady's last name is *Haddad*—does that ring a bell?"

"No."

"What was the name of the head of security at the museum?"

"Gershom Had . . . *Haddad!*"

"Right! And he never called me back or responded to my email, which makes me suspicious about his involvement in the heist. So, I wonder if that's his wife, and why she's leaving Israel, and why she seemed so curious about my time in England."

Afton turned toward him. "You *did* read Sherlock Holmes books, Dakota!"

"Well, I'm no Sherlock Holmes. But I'd *sure* like to *lock* up the *homies* who stole the artifacts and tried to kill us."

"Ah, I see what you did there. You're clever. What are you going to do?"

"I'm going to talk to her."

"Right now?"

"When we land."

To be continued.

In the next book, we'll find out:

- who this Mrs. Haddad is
- what happens when the families land in England
- if the other artifacts are discovered
- if the blossoming romance between Dakota and Afton continues
- what happens to Radomir, Ahmed, Eeman, and Avner

Would you like to receive an early copy of the next book before it's officially out? Did you enjoy the story? Let the author know by emailing:
abr@alwaysbeready.com

*Learn more about the author
and his other books at:*

AlwaysBeReady.com

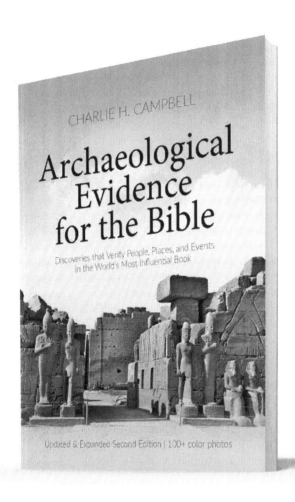